An Evil Surrender

"You have beaten me, Lan Martak," said Claybore without a hint of rancor. This more than anything else put Lan on guard. Claybore would never surrender. Not this easily. Not when there was a single spell yet to be cast, a single geas to be applied.

"Then I want proof of it!" shouted Lan. He blasted outward with the most devastating spell of which he was capable. Lan almost laughed aloud when he saw Claybore's skull begin to split in half.

Then he screamed. From within the skull came insects of all sizes and shapes. Pincers snapping, mosquito-stingers probing, the cloud of insects erupted forth and filled the entire chamber...

FIRE AND FOG

ROBERT E. VARDEMAN

ACE SCIENCE FICTION BOOKS
NEW YORK

FIRE AND FOG

An Ace Science Fiction Book/published by arrangement with
the author

PRINTING HISTORY
Ace Original/July 1984

ISBN: 0-441-23824-6

Ace Science Fiction Books are published by The Berkley Publishing Group,
200 Madison Avenue, New York, New York 10016.
PRINTED IN THE UNITED STATES OF AMERICA

For Bob Sullivan

WHEN YOU SELL OUT,
YOU MAKE EVERYONE HAPPY.

FIRE AND FOG

CHAPTER ONE

A warrior dressed in flame strode out. No human this, he towered a hundred feet above the walls of the fortress city of Wurnna. Immense hands clutched a ponderous sword that no score of men might lift. Muscles rippling and sending out dancing tongues of fire, the giant swung the weapon.

Lan Martak knew the defense of the city rested with him and him alone. He tried to ward off the blow, but the magical sword grated and screeched and cut through the stony battlement, sending vast clouds of dust into the air. Wherever the sword touched stone, it turned molten and burned with insane intensity. None of the mages of Wurnna approached closer than a bowshot; none could endure the searing flame.

The giant bellowed out his hatred for all within the city and took a mighty overhead swing. The blade sundered the wall with a deafening crash and sent molten droplets flying in deadly streams.

"Lan," cried his companion Inyx, "there is no stopping it. The spells aren't even slowing the monster." Lan reached out and gripped her hand, more for his own solace than to reassure her.

1

The young mage studied, probed, lightly tested Claybore's monster for some clue on how to defeat it. The disembodied sorcerer's attack was diabolically cunning. Lan, Inyx, and their spider friend Krek had chased the dismembered Claybore across the worlds along the Cenotaph Road, preventing him from regaining bodily parts severed and strewn eons ago by an even greater mage. But even with only head and torso intact, Claybore proved an adversary more than Lan's match.

Lan Martak began to worry that he would lose the battle for Wurnna, and with it what Claybore sought so diligently: the tongue resting within the Wurnnan ruler's mouth.

Lan clapped his hands and sent his familiar, a dancing mote of light, straight down into the ground at the giant's feet. The mote spun in ever-widening circles, boring, chewing up the very earth. Lan probed downward into the ground, summoning darkness to counter the flame. The pit widened and the burning giant was forced to retreat out of sword-range of the city.

"Lan," said Inyx, tugging at his sleeve. "The giant. There's something about him that's familiar."

"I know. It's Alberto Silvain, Claybore's commander in chief."

Inyx recoiled in shock, thinking Lan's exertions had somehow caused his mind to snap. Then she looked more carefully at the giant's features. Bloated, vastly out of proportion, hidden by curtains of fire, but still she saw the resemblance.

"It *is* Silvain," she said, awe tingeing her voice. Her hatred for the man and the way he had raped her caused Inyx to begin to tremble. She wanted Silvain to die—by her own hand.

The pit grew, Lan's powerful mote of light digging until the cavity stretched from one side of the canyon to the other, preventing the giant from crossing to again menace the city.

"Prepare to launch a bolt of pure energy directly at the

giant's feet," Lan ordered the few remaining mages huddling nearby. Sorcerers tended to be arrogant. But the spirit of the Wurnna mages had been broken long ago, first by their own ruler Iron Tongue and now by Claybore's incessant attacks, which none dared meet head-on. All Lan hoped for was some small additional backing. The brunt of this battle was his and his alone.

He turned and looked at the ruler of Wurnna, the man whom Claybore sought above all others on this world. Residing in his mouth was Claybore's magical tongue, a tongue whose slightest use commanded legions.

"Iron Tongue," whispered Inyx, "tell the giant to stand still. Don't let him move. You did it before. Do it again." She was heartened to see the demented ruler puff up and look out onto the battlefield. His understanding of reality had fled, but some tasks still pleasured him.

"Die!" cried Iron Tongue. The word exploded from his mouth, backed by the full power of the organ. Lan stumbled and had to support himself under the onslaught of that command. Iron Tongue might be insane, but the power of his magical tongue remained.

The effect on the giant convinced Lan that the battle might yet be theirs. He hadn't counted on the potent effects of the tongue Claybore so ardently sought to recover. The giant that was Alberto Silvain stumbled and lurched as if drunk on some heady wine. While still countering the force of Iron Tongue's command, the giant was vulnerable.

Lan Martak took full advantage to send the deadly bolt of energy the others had forged directly into Silvain's chest. The bolt appeared to be the largest lightning strike seen by humanity; to Lan it was a spear with a razor-sharp point driving straight for Silvain's heart. Not content with this, Lan diverted a bit of his power to further widen the vast cavity in the ground.

When the spear struck dead-center in his chest, Silvain let out a roar rivaling an erupting volcano. And, as from a volcano, torrents of hot lava rushed outward. This lava was the giant's lifeblood. Larger-than-life hands clutching vainly at the magical bolt piercing his flesh, Silvain sank to his knees.

"Martak," boomed the single name from his lips. It combined admiration, accusation, and condemnation all in that instant.

Lan widened the hole until the dirt began crumbling under Silvain's knees. The giant fought to stay upright on his knees, to avoid falling into the limitless pit in front of him.

"Martak," Silvain repeated, then convulsively heaved the immense sword at Wurnna's battlements. Lan took the opportunity to enlarge the bottomless hole a few inches further. The flaming giant fell forward into it, twisting and struggling, then grew smaller and smaller, cooler and smaller, finally vanishing from sight.

Lan let out a gasp of relief that was replaced by stark terror when he blinked and saw the thrown sword inexorably moving toward him. The weapon moved as if dipped in honey, but it moved.

Spells bounced off it. The dancing light mote couldn't touch it. Nothing deflected it.

"Out of the way," Lan commanded, knowing this might be Wurnna's doom. Claybore had counted on his attacking the wrong place. He had sacrificed his commander in chief in order to deliver this weapon. Silvain was a pawn now discarded; the sword carried magics Lan couldn't even guess at.

"I shall stop it," declared Iron Tongue. The ruler stood proudly on the battlement, chest bared as if daring Claybore to make the attempt. The sword moved smoothly, slowly, an unstoppable evil force.

Iron Tongue sucked in a lungful of air, then wove the command for the sword to vanish. It never wavered in its painstakingly slow journey toward Iron Tongue and the city of mages.

"Stop, I say. I command you. I am Iron Tongue. You can't ignore my command. Stop, *stop!*"

The huge sword point pierced Iron Tongue's chest. Like a branding iron through snow it came on, his flesh not even retarding the magical weapon's progress. Iron Tongue twitched and weakly fought, a new command on his lips. Mouth falling open in death, the sorcerer's tongue dangled out obscenely.

"It's aimed for me," Lan said, pushing Inyx away. "Go join the others. I don't want you close by."

"No, Lan, we're in this together."

He didn't argue. With a wave of his hand he conjured a shock wave that lifted her from her feet and tossed her off the battlements. She landed below in a pile of rubble. He couldn't even take the time to see if the fall had injured her. Even if it had, the fall was less likely to kill than the magical device he now faced.

The sword passed entirely through Iron Tongue, finally allowing the dead mage to slump to the stone walkway. As if guided by an unseen hand, the point turned and directed itself for Lan's midsection. Spell after spell he tried, all futilely. His mind worked at top speed, trying to understand what Claybore had done. Then he had it. The spells fell into their proper place; his hands moved in the proper orbits; the chants sounded right.

The sword struck.

Lan screamed, his concentration gone as excruciating pain lashed his senses. He jerked away as it pinked just under his eye and felt the sword dig deeper into his flesh, his bone. He grabbed at the sword blade with his hands, knowing even as he did so that no physical force would move the magical object from its course. The sword point dug deeper into cheek, burrowing into the jawbone, driving for the back of his head where the magical point might sever the spinal column.

Lan couldn't stop the deadly advance; the joined forces of the remaining mages of Wurnna did. Rugga, senior of those sorcerers surviving, built on what Lan had started, forging a parrying force that turned the blade at the last possible instant.

"Destroy it!" shrieked Rugga. "Destroy Claybore's evil sword!"

Her anger and hatred flowered and added supplemental power to the spell she had guided. Although weakened, the sorcerers found enough strength to shatter the blade. As it had sailed, so did it explode. Ruptured pieces turned slow cartwheels, barely moving, still deadly. Only when the last had embedded themselves harmlessly in stone or deep in the earth did Rugga and Inyx rush forward to tend to Lan.

"Oh, no, by all the Fates, no," Inyx said over and over. She stood in shock at the sight. The lower right portion of Lan's jaw had been sheared away, leaving his mouth a bloody ruin. Thick spurts of his life juices blossomed and washed down neck and chest.

"Claybore's revenge must be sweet," said Rugga, the bitterness there for all to hear. "He's cut out the tongue of his most powerful adversary. Lan Martak will never again utter a spell."

"Do something," pleaded Inyx. "He's dying." The woman's crude and usually effective first aid hadn't staunched the geysering flow of blood from Lan's jaw, where arteries had been clipped by the sword. He no longer made bubbling noises of pain. His body refused to believe such agony was possible and rejected any further misery, in preparation for death.

But Inyx felt it fully for him. He'd been a handsome man, young, vital, quick of wit and quicker with his friendship and love. Now he lay with the lower right half of his jaw cut away. His tongue had vanished along with bone and teeth and palate, making only deep-throated sounds possible now.

"He is dying," came the mocking words. "I can save him. Give me the tongue and I will save your lover." The image of Claybore's skull and torso floated a few feet away. Inyx knew this was only illusion, that the sorcerer remained safely hidden away where none might physically reach him.

The offer tempted her sorely. Lan's life for the worthless tongue in a dead mage's mouth. Then she heard soft rustlings of silk. She turned and saw the giant spider Krek mounting the perpendicular stone wall as if it had stairs cut into it. The soft sounds came from the coppery-bristled fur on his legs brushing as he walked.

"Friend Inyx," the spider said, "I feel as you do for our fallen friend, but what was his mission?"

"To stop Claybore," she said, her voice choked. Then, firmer with resolve, she glared at Claybore's fleshless skull and defiantly said, "Burn in all the Lower Places. You won't get the tongue!"

"He is dying. I can save him."

"He dies thwarting you. What more can any warrior ask? He died honorably, nobly, for a cause that means something."

"It means nothing!" roared the skull. "Nothing, do you hear!"

A wicked smile crossed Inyx's lips.

"You won't get the tongue. He stopped you. Dar-elLan-Martak stopped Silvain and now he's stopped you."

Claybore's response chilled her. She'd hoped for a moment of rage from the sorcerer. It didn't come. He laughed without humor.

"The tongue will be mine. You can't stop me now. Those few pitiful mages cannot conjure a fraction as well as I do. Silvain died for me. Do you think there are others any less willing? Are you ready to face still another giant?"

"While it might be true that your conjuration powers

exceed those shown by the Wurnna sorcerers," said Krek, "it is within their power to destroy the tongue before you can recover it. You shall lose its use, even if you do conquer this entire world. Of what use is such a pyrrhic victory?"

Again Claybore surprised them with his reaction.

He laughed louder, harder than ever before.

"The tongue is important, but I have won. Oh, yes, worms, I have won. He is dead." Ruby beams flashed from empty sockets to lightly brush across Lan's body. The man twitched, but could not cry out in pain. "More important, my agents on other worlds have been active. While you tried your pitiful efforts against me on this world, they have been successful elsewhere. Soon enough, arms and legs will be mine."

"You won't have a tongue!" taunted Inyx, but deep inside she felt sickness mounting. Their triumph seemed pathetic in the face of Claybore's victory. Destroying the tongue did not prevent him from becoming more powerful through the regaining of other bodily parts.

"I come for my tongue." The image vanished.

For long minutes none moved; then Rugga motioned for the other mages to join her.

"He must be healed," she said, indicating Lan's limp form. "Bringing the dead back to life is beyond our power, but saving a life might not be."

The mages chanted, hummed, made magical signs in the air that burned with fiery intensity and left the odor of brimstone, but Lan got no better. Inyx thought the slow consumption by death had been halted; but they did him no favors preserving him at this level. He had been a vital man, a vibrant one, full of life. To leave him like this was a travesty. Better she drive a dagger through his noble heart.

"Stay your hand, friend Inyx," said the spider. "There is one course of action you have not taken."

"What? What is it?" she demanded, eyes wide and imploring.

"I do not know if it will work, but it seems most logical. You see, there is a symmetry to the universe that we arachnids often ponder. Perhaps it comes from our love of geometrically symmetrical webs. We spin and weave and—"

"Krek!"

"Oh, yes. I shall try it and see." The spider lumbered over to Iron Tongue's body and used his front legs to roll the corpse onto its back. The dead mage's head lolled grotesquely to one side, the tongue so eagerly sought by Claybore thrusting from between bloated lips. Krek used his front talons to separate the lips and open the mouth. Bending down until the serrated tips of his mandibles were deep inside, he snipped.

The spider jumped back, a shrill screech piercing the air. The contact with the magical tongue had caused blue sparks to erupt forth, burning both dead lips and living spider. But Krek held the organ between his powerful mandibles. Spinning in place, he pushed through the mages and placed the tongue into the sundered oral cavity of his friend.

"It is yours by right," Krek said softly. "Yours is the destiny we must all follow and aid. Use the magic to heal yourself. Do it, friend Lan Martak. We need you!"

A tear formed at the corner of his saucer-sized eye. Inyx gently wiped it away as she hugged one of his thick middle legs and watched.

For minutes nothing happened; then Rugga jerked back, a look of surprise on her face.

"Our magics are blocked. We can no longer aid him. He . . . he is healing himself."

Inyx dared to hope then. More minutes passed and a startling transformation began. What had been bone once in Lan's face became bone again. Whitely exposed, it gleamed in the pale light of the setting sun. Then it was no longer visible. Skin flowed and covered it, recreating Lan's normal visage. But the young mage lay as still as death.

"Help him now," urged Inyx. "Give him your strength."

"He blocks us. All of us together cannot pierce the cloak he pulls about himself."

Then came the faint and eerie chants from Lan's newly grown lips. The spell mounted in power, built and soared to the skies. It was a spell of power and hope and success.

His soft brown eyes flickered open and met Inyx's vivid blue ones.

"Lan?" she said hesitantly, unsure of herself, unsure of Lan.

"It'll be all right. The tongue. It... it's giving me power I never thought possible. The spells I only half-understood. They're crystal clear to me now. And more! I see so much more!"

Turning to Rugga, Inyx asked, "What effect will that tongue have on him? When Iron Tongue confronted Claybore, it drove him mad. Because the tongue was once Claybore's, might that not happen with Lan, also?"

Rugga only shrugged. She was the most potent sorcerer in Wurnna now, but this was far beyond her expertise. Compared with Claybore—and Lan Martak—she was only an apprentice.

"Claybore still remains," pointed out Krek. "From what the skull has said, victory on this world is minor. Should not our attentions be directed elsewhere?"

"Claybore is on this world," Lan said. "I 'feel' him nearby. If he is stopped now, the war is won." He got to his feet with Inyx's strong arm around his shoulders for support. He tapped into the power stone around him, allowed the tongue to roll in his mouth, he drenched with his saliva, become a part of his body—and soul.

"He still wants the tongue," said warrior captain Jacy Noratumi. "But now we can fight him for it. You can do it, Martak. You can!"

Lan said nothing. He waited, consolidating the power building within, savoring the richness of his senses, the nearness of his own death. When Claybore came, he was ready.

"The tongue!" demanded Claybore.

"Your death," said Lan in a voice so soft it was barely audible. But he did not merely speak, he used the Voice. "I want you to slay yourself. Kill yourself, Claybore. Die, *die!*" He put all the urgency possible into that command.

And Claybore started to obey.

Only a faint human voice crying out broke the spell and saved Claybore's quasi-existence.

Claybore trembled all over, shaking down to the mechanical legs bearing him.

"You have my tongue. You shall pay for this insult, Martak. You will wish you had died from my sword!"

Again came the human voice, clearer now, distinct, and belonging to Claybore's new commander, Kiska k'Adesina.

"All is ready, Master. Hurry. We must go. My mage Patriccan can hold them back no longer. The troops are mutinying."

"I told your bitch," Claybore roared at Lan. "I tell you. This only seems victory for you. On other worlds, I have triumphed. When next we meet, do not think the battle will be so gentle."

Lan formed the most potent spell he knew and sent the bolt of energy blazing for Claybore. The leading edge of the energy spear wavered for an instant, then found only emptiness.

"Claybore has shifted worlds," moaned Inyx. "He has walked the Road."

"And there aren't any cenotaphs nearby," said Krek. "I 'see' one within a month's travel time, and I am not sure where it leads. It might be onto another world, altogether different from the one chosen by Claybore."

"If we don't hurry and follow him, he'll regain arms and legs and become too powerful even for you, Lan."

"A cenotaph," mused the young mage. "We can create

one out there, on the plain in front of Wurnna."

"I suppose there are some bodies lost, but don't you need to know the name for the consecration? It'll take weeks to determine who has died and which corpses are which. Oh, Lan, that'll take as long as hiking to the cenotaph Krek 'sees.'"

"We think in terms far too narrow. What to us is a hero is to our enemies a villain."

"So?"

"It is true the other way, also. A villain to us is a hero to our enemies."

"I don't see—no, Lan. You can't do this. I *hate* him. I was angry when you denied me the chance to kill him."

"You would consecrate a cenotaph to Alberto Silvain?" asked Krek. "What a novel idea."

"There is more to it than novelty, Krek. Silvain's fortunes were linked intimately with Claybore's. Properly done, the cenotaph will continue to join their fortunes—and this world with the one chosen by Claybore. It is the only way we have of finding him among the myriad worlds along the Road."

Lan Martak left them behind to walk slowly to the edge of the black pit he had formed. Into this vortex of darkness Silvain had fallen. The flames of his life had been snuffed out for all eternity and his body irretrievably lost in a fashion not even Lan Martak understood. Perhaps the all-knowing Resident of the Pit might have been able to trace Silvain's course through the universe, but the Resident resided on Lan's home world, many worlds away.

Lan's hand rested on the closed grimoire he carried within his tunic. After a moment's pause, he knew he had no need to refresh his memory about the summoning spell or the proper method of consecration.

He began the chant, now surprisingly easy when uttered with the tongue that had once belonged to Claybore.

*   *   *

Krek pointed with his long front leg. "The cenotaph opens."

"Silvain," muttered Inyx, remembering the foul deeds Claybore's commandant had committed. But Lan had been correct. Silvain's courage in assuming the magical guise given by Claybore to attack an entire city filled with sorcerers had been strong enough to open the pathway between worlds.

"Ready?" asked Lan Martak.

"Is this truly the world where Claybore walks?"

The mage shrugged his shoulders. His powers had grown, but there were some—many—questions he had no answer for.

"Let us leave this fine world behind," said Krek. The spider boldly entered the simple stone cairn, wavered for a moment, and vanished from sight.

Lan Martak took Inyx's hand, squeezed, and then led the way. They too shimmered as if caught in summer heat, felt the gut-wrenching shift to another world, then came out ready to pursue their adversary.

They walked the Cenotaph Road hand in hand, only to emerge on a windswept, dark plain on a different world. Only rocky expanse and jagged, cloud-crowned black mountains in the distance were visible.

Everywhere there was the smell of . . . burning.

"Looks like rain," said Inyx, glancing up at the lead-heavy clouds swirling overhead.

"Rain!" cried Krek. "I shall surely die!"

Lan started to laugh, but the laugh turned to a cry of anguish when the first raindrop struck his flesh and it began to char.

CHAPTER TWO

"Claybore attacks!" screamed Krek, his voice carrying the tone of pure anguish. The spider jumped about, rubbing one massive leg against another in a vain attempt to remove the droplets of acid burning through his fur.

"It's not Claybore's doing," said Lan Martak, shielding his face from the sporadic raindrops falling from the clouds. He winced as a droplet heavy with acid spattered wetly over his protecting hand and onto his face.

"I burn!"

The spider's fur had begun to smolder from the falling acid. In his fruitless attempt to avoid the rain, Krek even rolled on the ground. Lan saw instantly that this made it worse. Every spot the rain touched caused the rock to burst into a tiny fountain of flame. Looking out over the barren plain, he saw minute watchfires springing up with greater frequency. When the rain began to pour down in a full storm, the entire world might be set ablaze.

Inyx saw this and said to Lan, "We've got to find cover. Left out here, it won't matter what Claybore can or can't do to us. The elements will burn or boil us."

15

Lan closed his eyes and let his mind wander. When he found the dancing light that had become his companion, he enticed it closer, teasing, cajoling, promising. The familiar burst overhead and spread out an umbrella of pure energy to protect the trio from the increasingly vigorous acidfall.

"Now, Krek," the young warrior mage said, "let's see to putting out your fires."

"Water! Fire! I drown and burn! This is the worst of all possible worlds. Why did I ever leave fair Wurnna behind? I could have made peace with Murrk and the other spiders. They'd let me stay high in the webs, swinging in the gentle breezes. But no, I walk the Road and find *both* fire and water to confound me!"

"Lan, he does need help," said Inyx. She furrowed her brow in worry as huge patches of coppery fur on the spider's legs began turning into charcoal and falling off in gobs. "He won't be able to endure much more of this."

Lan rubbed his hands together, then let his fingers trace out a fiery pattern that hung suspended in the air. The pattern took on new shapes and burned with an intensity equal to that of the rocks silently erupting into flame all around. Spinning, the pattern became nothing more than a blur, then sped directly for the spider.

Krek let forth a shrill scream of almost human agony, then vented one of his gusty, spiderish sighs. He shook for a moment, then stood on all eight legs.

"Whatever you did, friend Lan Martak, thank you. The burning is gone. But my poor fur...." Krek's head craned around and studied the damage done to his fine leg fur.

"It'll grow back, Krek. Just wait and see," soothed Inyx.

While the pair of them talked in low tones, Lan walked to the edge of the protection formed by his magical umbrella and peered out at the landscape. Seldom had he seen such a foreboding place. The watchfires sputtered and leaped wherever the acid rain touched—but he did see a narrow path leading off into the cloud-obscured distance. Occasional gusts of wind cleared the horizon to reveal a towering mountain wrapped in a flame envelope. Other than this, the world appeared denuded of all contour.

"Not even vegetation," he mused, looking over the terrain. Lan realized this might mean nothing. After all, they had emerged on this world in the center of a graveyard. Around him stood small marker stones commemorating the passing of dozens of lost souls. The cenotaph from which they'd emerged was even more poorly marked, giving it the aspect of a pauper's grave. The more he looked around, the more Lan warmed to the idea that this was a potter's field where the indigent were lain to whatever rest they could find.

"Any sign of Claybore?" asked Inyx, coming to his side and putting a gentle hand around his waist.

"Magically, I haven't tried. I fear any use of a scrying spell might alert him."

"The umbrella won't draw his attention?" Fearfully, she looked above to where the acid rain pelted down onto the thin magical sheet stretched taut.

"There are hints of magic all around. This won't command any more attention than the others. But you are right. We must keep the use of my spells to a minimum or we will warn him of our presence. Surprise is our greatest ally at the moment."

"You've grown in your powers so much I hardly know what you can and can't do," she said, her voice strained.

He missed the tone.

"Claybore's power is still greater. And if he finds his arms and legs on this world, there will be no stopping him."

"The tongue won't stand against him?"

"I . . . I don't know," Lan admitted. He rolled the iron organ about in his mouth. It carried with it a metallic taste, but other than this he might as well have had his natural tongue. But the young mage knew the power of the tongue. He had seen the commands given for suicide followed instantly and without question. The tongue enhanced a spell, gave him the Voice, made him much, much more than he had been.

And in some fashion he didn't understand, it allowed him to more closely understand Claybore. This tongue had once been a part of that renegade mage; now that it rested inside Lan's mouth, the two were merged in a subtle and magical way.

"Where is he? Can you tell without the scrying spell?"

"No, I can't," he told his raven-haired companion. Lan looked into Inyx's brilliant blue eyes and saw concern there, concern for him. "About all I can find is what my senses tell me."

"We already know this is a terrible place," moaned Krek. "An awful place full of vile things. Oh, woe! Why did I leave my web and my lovely bride Klawn?"

Lan ignored the spider's lamentations.

"There's nothing to be seen except for the peak rising yonder." He pointed it out to Inyx when another strong gust of wind cleared away the veiling fog around it.

"Don't be so sure. Lower your sights a little. There, over to the right." Inyx pointed. Lan followed the sleek line of her arm to a spot not a hundred yards away.

"Interesting. They seem to be digging a grave," he said.

"Robbing it is my guess. Who else would dare the wretched elements on this planet but grave robbers?"

"Quiet, Krek. Let's go see if we can strike up a conversation and learn something of this place."

"I do not wish to speak to anyone. Not if they are native to this horrid place," the spider said, sulking.

"Then you'll sit in the middle of the rain. The umbrella comes with me."

Lan whistled, gestured, and started off. The glowing protective sheet sailed several feet above his head. Inyx kept pace and Krek saw that he had to, also, or end up out in the searing acid rain. The arachnid lumbered along, grumbling as he went.

"Good day," called out Lan from a safe distance. The gravediggers barely stood four feet tall and were immensely powerful. Wrists as thick as Lan's forearm twisted shovels and spades in the rocky soil. Their noses were bulbous like potato sprouts and the gnarly ears protruding from the sides of their misshapen heads looked to be more vegetable than animal in origin. One of the diggers turned a rheumy eye toward Lan, but other than this, none paid him the slightest attention.

"Sociable crew, aren't they?" commented Inyx.

"You try," urged Lan. "Sometimes you can strike up a conversation better than I can."

Inyx tried and failed. The four gnomes continued digging until they had a grave a half-dozen feet deep and two by five across the rocky plain.

"Mayhaps they are incapable of speaking," said Krek. "Or perhaps they are merely rude little buggers."

"Rude!" blared the one Lan took to be the leader. "We're not rude! How dare you offend us by saying such a vile thing? The Heresler clan is more polite than any of the others—all the others taken together! Ask any of us!"

"Did we offend you?" asked Lan. "There are many differences in cultures."

"You didn't offend me. You? Either of you two fools?" The leader took a quick inventory of his men and shook his head. Hair the diameter and texture of seaweed fluttered over his eyes. He pushed the greasy hair back into uneasy equilibrium without even noticing he did so.

"Allow me to introduce . . ." Lan began.

"Who cares who you are? We have work to do."

"And he thinks he's not rude. Wonder what the others are like?" asked Inyx.

"Others? You have contact with the Tefize?"

"What could it matter to you?" asked Lan.

The gnome threw down his shovel and stomped over to stand less than six inches away from Lan. Chin thrusting upward, hands on broad hips, the gnome glared at Lan.

"They are sworn enemies. Do you have dealings with the Tefize or not?"

"No." Lan used just the slightest amount of the Voice with his answer. Inyx cringed when she felt the power radiating outward. The gnome hardly took note of it. He only nodded briskly.

"Good."

He turned to go back to his digging.

"Wait!" Lan's patience was nearing an end. "We want information. We need shelter, we need food, we want to find out if another has come this way. We need a lot of things."

"Who doesn't?"

Lan had grown up on a forested world where hunting provided the major means of his sustenance. Patience had become inbred with him. To lie in a tree over a game trail waiting for the right-sized doe or buck, then to leap down like an attacking pard required skill and determination and . . . patience.

Since his magical powers grew, Lan Martak found his temper increasingly short-fused.

"Krek, eat them. All four."

"Lan!" protested Inyx. He gripped her arm to silence her outburst.

The four gnomes exchanged worried looks—or what Lan thought were worried looks.

The leader barked out, "Get back to work. We have to finish before nightfall."

When one of the others saw Krek advancing and looked up at the eight-foot-tall, eight-legged horror, he swung his shovel as hard as he could. The blade smashed into the back of his leader's head. The gnome crashed face down into the grave he was digging, never uttering a sound.

"I'm leader now," spoke up the one who had so creatively used his shovel. "Let's negotiate this."

"Now we're getting somewhere," said Lan. "Come, sit beside us so we can talk." He didn't want to tower over the gnome. Such difference in position lent an air of uneasiness to the one being looked down upon, or so Lan had found in his experience. The gnome plopped down and crossed his arms, looking expectantly at Lan to begin.

"We are travelers along the Cenotaph Road," he began.

"Yes, yes," said the gnome impatiently. "That much is obvious. Who else but traveler or a Heresler would be out in the graveyard? Certainly not the Tefize or the Kaan or the Willikens, damn them all. So. You have to be walking the Road."

Lan frowned. While many peoples along the Road knew of the existence of other worlds, few took it so casually.

"Why don't you walk the Road yourself and get away from all this?" Lan gestured to encompass the downpour of acidic rain. Every drop touched off a tiny explosion now, leaving behind a pocked and flaming crater. To be caught unprotected on that plain meant certain death, and even under his magical umbrella, he sensed a new danger. The air filled with noxious gases released by the flaming rocks.

"This is home. Why wander?" asked the gnome, obviously puzzled at the question. Lan didn't pursue the matter further. Perdition to one was paradise to another.

"My name is Lan Martak, this is Inyx, and the big one is Krek."

"Krek-k'with-kritklik," spoke up Krek, "but the human palate does not seem adequate for the task of pronouncing a real name."

The gnome made a noise like he spat, then said, "I see why they call you Krek. I am Broit Heresler, head of the Heresler clan."

"Head?" asked Inyx in surprise. She glanced over at the

gnome struggling to sit up in the grave. He rubbed the back of his head where Broit had smashed him with the shovel.

"Oh, damn," said Broit, springing to his feet. He scooped up his shovel and again smashed the fallen gnome in the back of the head. He added one last whack to make sure of the job, tossed down the shovel, and returned to sit by Lan.

"Promotion is swift on this planet," muttered Lan.

"He was a tyrant, anyway," said Broit Heresler. "And he did absolutely nothing to fend off the Tefize. They are walking all over us. Imagine. They denigrate the position of us gravediggers in polite society."

"What function do the Tefize play?"

"They don't do anything but cart around food and shit and stuff like that. Imagine. They never even leave the confines of the Home and they have the nerve to say we're deadbeats."

"Anyone leaving the safety of, uh, the Home to come out here is hardly that," agreed Lan.

"I like you," said Broit. "You're quick on the uptake."

"Thank you. Tell me about the Tefize. How long has your clan and theirs been at odds?"

Broit looked at the young mage and shook his head. He made an ugly face and then spat onto the ground. Where the gobbet hit, a thin column of steam rose. Lan wondered if the acid rain caused the fire or whether it merely acted as a catalyst and any moisture would suffice to produce the blazes.

"Generations. Longer. It's always that way. The doers pitted against the takers. Bodies'd build up sky high if it wasn't for us. Who else is there to carry out the dead and put them in the ground where they belong?"

"Keeps you busy," said Inyx.

"Damn right it does. The Hereslers perform vital service."

"When did the tide begin to go against you?" asked Lan.

"What makes you think it has been?" demanded Broit. "I never said anything about anything going wrongo. Not in the least."

"A guess."

"Maybe a month, maybe two. If you ask me—and you can now, since I'm clan chieftain—it's that mage the Tefize recruited. He's been making mischief all over the place." Broit spat once more.

"The disembodied mage?" asked Lan, trying to sound as casual as possible. He felt electricity surging throughout his body. Most of all, his tongue tingled with the need to demand of this gnome the truth. Such a use of magic would certainly bring unwanted attention from Claybore; Lan fought down the urge.

"He's the one. Another walker along the Road. Damn fool doesn't have any legs. Uses a mechanical gadget to get about on. No arms, either, but it doesn't seem to bother him a whole lot. He's around, but he's not the one causing all the fuss."

"The woman with him is probably the one, right?" asked Inyx.

"You folks know where all the bodies are hidden, that's for sure," said Broit. "Kiska k'Adesina, they call her. What a bitch. Always getting into trouble and making a mess. She's increased the Heresler work load tenfold since she showed up." Broit rubbed over his bent back to show how much gravedigging had increased since Claybore's new commandant had arrived.

"Are there many of the grey-clad soldiers about?"

"Who? No soldiers, not since we killed off the last of the Larsh clan some sixty years ago. Buried every last one of them, we did. Some were still alive when we did, too. Served 'em right."

"What would happen if the Tefize are victorious in this civil war you're waging?" asked Lan.

Broit Heresler shrugged.

"Would they wipe out all of the Hereslers?"

"Sure would. In a snap." Broit wound up, harumphed, and spat a good ten feet, watching the spittle attract acid droplets as it flew. By the time it hit the ground, it virtually exploded like a small artillery shell.

"You don't seem overly concerned with this," said Inyx. "Wouldn't you like a bit of help to prevent being killed?"

"Wouldn't turn it down," said the gnome. "Wouldn't want to accept it, either. Big load to carry when you start taking favors from people. Look at what'll happen to the Tefize. This Claybore will take them for a bunch, count on it."

"If you are no longer around, what matters it to you?" asked Krek.

"Everyone's got to go sometime. Nobody knows that better'n a gravedigger, righto?"

"I suppose so," said Lan.

"Got to finish up," said Broit, peering out from under the magical umbrella at the overcast sky. "If we don't, we're going to get caught in the fog. Wouldn't want to be cut off from Yerrary, no way."

"Yerrary?" asked Lan. "Is that the mountain I saw?"

"More'n any mountain you ever saw. That's Home."

"But the mountain's name is Yerrary?"

"Well," said the gnome, obviously thinking hard on the subject, "it is and it isn't. Yerrary's the name of our major deity, not that anybody worships her any more. But we still use the name for Home. Seemed right at the time. Now, who cares? We're all dead sooner or later."

"That we are," said Inyx.

"You two get digging. And cover him up. I don't want him coming around again. Hate to bend the shovel more'n I have already." Broit sat and supervised while the other two gnomes diligently worked in the acid rain to dig three more graves and to cover over the one in which their onetime leader lay.

Lan almost protested, then stopped himself. Different cultures, different customs. Broit appeared to be an amiable enough sort, whereas his predecessor hadn't been. They'd need all the aid they could get to fight off Claybore and Kiska k'Adesina. Alliance with the Heresler clan might not be enough, but it gave them a starting point.

"Enough for the day. Got to go." Broit rose and stalked off, the acid rain hardly bothering him, even though tiny pieces of his shirt burned away as he went.

"A moment, Broit," called Lan. "Might we accompany you?"

"Why?"

"We'd like to see Yerrary—Home."

"Do as you please."

"And we'd like to align ourselves in support of your fight against the Tefize. Claybore is our enemy, also."

"That doesn't mean the Tefize necessarily are. The enemy of my enemy isn't always my friend."

Lan wondered at the society forming such an obdurate philosophy, but he pressed onward. He needed to gain entry into Yerrary with the least possible disturbance. He had no doubt that k'Adesina already had posted guards on the entry points to prevent easy access. And once inside, the mountain passages probably went for miles—hundreds of miles. A sympathetic guide would aid them considerably.

"It is true this time. I would destroy every member of the Tefize to stop Claybore."

"Bloodthirsty bugger, aren't you? Well, come along. I'll think on it as we go." Broit nervously glanced around, checking the clouds, then studying a timepiece fastened to his wrist. "Time's a'wasting. Hurry it up."

The three gnomes set out at a pace belying their short legs. Lan and Inyx found it difficult to keep up with them and even Krek once muttered a spiderish curse about the poor footing.

"Why hurry so?" Lan asked Broit.

"Fog's coming in. Want to be inside the mountain before sundown."

"You mean this isn't nighttime?"

"Bright as day," he was assured by the gnome. "At sunset's when the fog rolls in. Damn stuff."

Lan maintained the umbrella overhead although he worried about its being detected as they neared the mountain. Yerrary rose up from the plain a full mile or more, its sides deeply eroded and here and there sporting jagged prominences showing where the gnomes had placed structures of their own. As he neared, the young mage saw tiny windows glowing with warm yellow light. Doorways dotted the entire mountainside and he knew there would be no way for k'Adesina to guard every one of them.

She would have to rely on the Tefize spy network for information—and that might take long hours to filter up to her. And if the Tefize were as uncooperative as the Hereslers appeared, she might never hear of his entry. Lan felt hope flaring. A quick entry, an even quicker attack, and victory was his!

"Even the mountain burns," grumbled Krek. "Look at it!"

As the rains cascaded over the rocky slopes and ran down gulleys, ten-foot-thick pillars of fire rose to gut the sky.

"There," said Broit, pointing with his stubby arm. "There's our way in."

A single door stood ajar at the base of the mountain. Lan collapsed his magical umbrella and sent the dancing mote of light forward to reconnoiter. It spun crazily and obediently whirled back to him, reporting no traps.

"Lan," said Inyx, her voice oddly pitched. "The fog. Look how it rolls down the side of the mountain. I've never seen anything like it before."

The fog formed claws and scratched at bare rock. Flaming paths were left behind as the fog crept ever downward.

Seeing this caused Broit and the other gnomes to break into a dead run.

"Why do they fear the fog?" Lan wondered aloud. "They certainly didn't seem to mind the rain burning away their clothing and flesh."

The fog billowed and roiled as if it had a life of its own. Lan and Inyx reached the doorway and turned to see Krek struggling to join them. A single feathery digit of fog cut the spider off from the doorway, almost as if the mist had a mind of its own.

"Krek?" called Lan. Something snapped inside the man. His tone changed and he used the Voice. "Krek! Come here immediately! Follow my voice. Now!"

"Lan, what's wrong?" Inyx asked anxiously.

Krek came through the fog, mandibles clacking. He roared a battle cry and charged them, intent on destruction. From the way his dun-colored eyes glazed over, it was obvious that he had gone berserk.

"Kill everyone!" screeched the giant spider as he bore down on Lan and Inyx.

CHAPTER THREE

"Stop him, Lan! He's gone crazy!" Inyx barely dodged the rampaging spider. Krek's mandibles clacked savagely just over her head. A lock of her lustrous dark hair went flying. Inyx dived forward and tried to stop him, but the spider's ponderous bulk proved too much for her. Inyx was dragged along and then tossed off as easily as Krek might rid himself of a small mite crawling on his leg.

"Krek, stop," said Lan Martak. He used the Voice, putting full magical power behind it. To his surprise, Krek didn't even slow. It was as if the spider hadn't heard.

"STOP!" he roared. The very slopes of the mountain behind rumbled with the command. The three gnomes who had preceded them into Yerrary spun and froze to the spot. The Voice, backed by all of Lan's magical skills, worked to perfection with them.

Krek continued to hack and slash and menace anyone drawing close to him. The arachnid was totally out of control.

"What's happened to him?" cried Inyx. She wiped a

bloody smear off her cheek where she'd been scratched during her brief attempt to slow Krek.

"The fog," muttered Broit Heresler, pointing. Lan saw tendrils of the fog billowing about, forming an almost solid figure, then seeping upward, seductively, slowly, inexorably toward them.

"What about it?" he demanded.

"The fog is a killer. You've no wish to be in it. Look what it did to the long-legged one."

Lan formed his protective barrier, again using the light mote familiar. But again to his surprise, the barrier presented no hindrance at all to the fog. It came on, oozing around and even through. He took a moment to check the fog's composition, hoping to find this was only an illusion sent by Claybore to confound and harass.

The fog was real, nothing more than water droplets held in a fine cloud.

"Has the acid burned through his fur and driven him insane?" asked Inyx, huddling close to Lan. She feared nothing, but knew from her futile attempt to stop Krek that there was no more she could do. The mage had to perform what, to her, looked like a miracle.

"The rain has stopped. There's only the fog," said Lan, trying to figure out what was happening. Claybore was innocent of this. There was no acid sear to drive Krek wild. What was it?

"The fog's a killer, it is," said Broit. "Get in out of it. You'll never rescue the big one. Righto?" he said, turning to the other two gnomes. Their gnarly hands tried to hide their faces; they succeeded so well all Lan saw was their abused vegetable ears sticking out on either side. He realized they were still under his command to stop. He freed them with a single pass. The pair ran off into the bowels of the mountain, safely Home.

Broit remained behind.

"Go, too," urged Lan. "This is our problem."

"It'll be mine if you don't cut him down. Think how many corpses that one can create if left alone. You'll need someone to tag the bodies properly and make sure they get the right grave site."

"What is it about the fog?" asked Lan, even as he performed another, more intricate spell to slow Krek's berserker rage. The spell failed, also.

"Doesn't look to be much, does it? The fog's got *things* in it."

"What sort of things? Living?"

Broit Heresler shrugged his hunched shoulders. Licking his lips nervously, he began pointing outward.

"See there and there? The fog comes on like it has a mind of its own. Who knows why it seeks out people, but it does. Then it drives them bonko, right out of their wits."

"There is nothing alive in the fog," said Lan. His magical explorations of the fog turned up nothing. "It must be a chemical, just as the rain was acid."

"Take one sniff of that fog and you'll be like he is." Broit Heresler backed through the entryway when Krek circled around and again came for them. The giant spider saw nothing. His path was dictated by the terrain and nothing more. He fought unseen enemies and if a friend happened in the way, that friend died.

"He doesn't have an inkling of what he's doing," said Lan. "The fog. Does it come off the mountain?"

"Of course it does," said Broit. "The rains set the mountainside on fire, then the fog drifts down, usually reaching its worst at sunset or sunrise."

"Some chemical enters the fog and is carried along on ordinary water drops. If inhaled, it acts as a mind-twisting drug."

"How's that help Krek, even if it is true?" asked Inyx. Lan held the woman back. She obviously tensed to make another attempt to tackle the eight-legged juggernaut.

"Watch."

Lan closed his eyes and forced his dancing mote of light into another shield. This time he kept it dense enough to prevent even the smallest of air particles from passing the membrane. The sheet of light spun and whirled and dropped like a net over the caroming spider. Krek fought it, slashing helplessly at it. While the scintillant sheet did nothing to stay his reckless running, it completely shut off the air.

"I made a mistake in not knowing the fog's nature," said Lan. "Remember in the tunnel leading to Wurnna how I prevented the power stone dust from reaching us?"

Inyx nodded but kept a careful eye on Krek. The spider still rolled and clawed and snapped viciously, but those actions were becoming weaker and weaker as oxygen-deprivation began.

"I kept the light shield so that air passed but larger dust particles didn't. I tried the same thing at first with Krek. Now I shut off all flow either in or out of the shield. I have him encapsulated."

"A bug in amber. How nice," said Broit Heresler. "Can I dig the grave for him when he suffocates? Never had to do one this big. Course, there was the mass burial we Hereslers did about thirty years back. I wasn't around to personally view it, but the grave was big, and I mean *big*. Everyone's still talking about it. The stuff of legends, don't you know?"

"There won't be a grave. As soon as he collapses, I'll release the shield and we can drag him inside. The fog doesn't enter Yerrary, does it?"

"We have tight doors."

Krek rolled onto his back and all eight legs kicked spastically. Ever weaker, the spider eventually lay without moving.

"Don't let him die, Lan," said Inyx, her fingers digging into the mage's arm.

"You know I won't. I'm going to have to put the shield around us. No air to breathe except what we start with, so move fast. Ready, now!"

Lan and Inyx ran out, hidden behind the impervious shield of light. Each grabbed one of Krek's thick legs and started to pull. Before they got halfway back to the entrance to the mountain fastness, Lan felt himself growing weaker, lightheaded, almost to the point of passing out.

"You're doing a better job at this than I am," he told Inyx. "I'll hold the shield around you alone to give more air. I'll follow."

"Lan, the fog's coming back."

"Get Krek inside. Do it!"

Lan rearranged the spell so that only Inyx remained inside the protective bubble of magic. The instant he freed himself, air gusted into his straining lungs. Gratefully, he dropped to his knees and sucked in huge draughts of life-giving oxygen. In the distance he heard Broit Heresler screeching about the fog.

Turning, Lan saw filmy tendrils reaching out for him. He smiled. These weren't foggy tendrils, these were a woman's fingers. A lovely woman caressing his face, beckoning him on. He stood and stared into the fog. It parted like a curtain in a theatre, revealing the most gorgeous creature Lan had ever seen.

Not quite human, she possessed a beauty transcending the physical.

"Come to me," she urged. Long fingers reached out to stroke and entice. Lan moved toward her. "I want you for my own. Together we can be invincible. Together, we can be gods."

"I'd like that," said Lan, moving away from the mountain and into the ethereal woman's embrace. But he did not find it. She danced away lightly, taunting him, leading him on.

"Come," she whispered seductively. "Come and I will grant you all your wishes."

"Stop Claybore," he said.

"That, yes. I can give you that."

"Inyx. Be with Inyx."

"You choose another woman over me? What a man! You can have us both. Come, come!"

He followed. He heard a faint cry from behind, but he ignored it. How could he be burdened with petty conversation when he was being promised universes?

Lan fell heavily onto his face when something smashed into the back of his knees.

"Dammit, Lan, the fog's got you, too!" came the cry.

Angry at being denied his ultimate fantasies, he kicked out. Inyx hung on with grim tenacity.

"Back, Lan. Fight it. The fog's burning away your brain. I can't hold out much longer. Hurry, Lan. Fight it!"

Inyx gasped out the last of her pent-up breath, imploring Lan to action. The sight of the lovely woman clinging to his leg, her face red with exertion, shook him.

"I need you," came the siren's call from the fog. "Leave her. I can give you anything—everything!"

Lan's brain churned and felt as if it would rip from his skull.

"Lan," wheezed Inyx, slowly succumbing to the fog's induced dreams. "It's Reinhardt. But it can't be. Vision, image. Not real. I remember being fooled before. Not real."

The mention of Inyx's dead husband snapped Lan back to a semblance of command over his emotions, his body. Reaching deep within, he summoned the most powerful magics of which he was capable. A small spire rose, spun, turned into a vortex catching the foggy tendrils within. The air elemental boiled about, shrieking with insane joy as Lan released it from eternal bondage.

The elemental spun to the sky and blasted itself free, taking with it most of the fog. Lan stood with the wind whipping around, snapping at his clothes, clawing at his face, and sucking out the moisture. He endured and the fog's effects faded.

"Come on, Inyx. Summoning the air elemental warned Claybore. It had to. That was potent magic, but nothing else seemed to work."

He half-dragged her back to where Broit Heresler stood in the doorway leading into the mountain. Beside him crouched Krek, shaking and openly crying.

"Why did I ever leave my fair young bride to walk the Road? Oh, Klawn, can you ever forgive me?"

"Shut up, Krek," commanded Lan. The spider's head snapped around when he saw Lan pulling Inyx inside. Broit slammed and locked the door. Lan noted with some satisfaction the rubber seals all around to prevent the fog from entering Yerrary.

"Give us a few minutes to rest, Broit. Then we can be on our way."

"Never seen anybody get away from the fog before. Don't know what it does, but it's a killer. Usually find the bodies miles from here. What a chore, dragging them to the graveyard. Can't just leave them in a nice pile by the door, no way. Nothing's ever that easy, even death." Broit cocked his head to one side and peered at Lan. "You're damn good. Think you can get rid of the Tefize and their pet sorcerer?"

"I'm going to try."

"Don't know what good that's going to do me. Just cause more work. Bodies, bodies everywhere! That's all that happens when we have a couple tame mages to do our fighting for us."

Lan Martak rested and closely watched both Krek and Inyx. The spider threw off the effects of the fog rapidly enough, but Inyx took longer. As she gasped for air, Lan considered the psychic effects he'd felt. Visions weren't produced by another, as when Claybore sent his nightmares to haunt Lan's sleep. Rather, these were images generated by the individual. He had no idea what Krek had seen, but it had terrified the spider. His own goals were all promised, if only he follow. And Inyx had again been shown her dead husband Reinhardt.

Lan smiled without humor. That image had been used to imprison the woman before, on another world, by a human mage without a shred of conscience or decency. Inyx had remembered and had used it to counter the fog's insidious effects long enough for Lan to recover and act.

He stroked over Inyx's raven hair, noting the spot where Krek's mandibles had cut a lock free. She no longer fought. He hummed quietly, soothingly. Of all the people he had met along the Cenotaph Road, of all the friends he had made, she was truly special.

Inyx was more than a friend to him. Much more.

Lan closed his eyes and sent forth his dancing light mote to scout through Yerrary. There was no need to play coy now. Claybore had to have sensed the prodigious powers released by the air elemental as it sucked up all the fog in its wild bid for freedom. The magical battle would soon be joined and he might as well know Claybore's location.

To his surprise, Lan found not only evidence of Claybore, but also of another mage, one nearly as powerful.

His eyes flashed open and focused on Broit.

"Are there other mages in Yerrary?" he asked.

"None left in the sorcerer's clan," said Broit. "Damn Lirory Tefize. When the sorcerers wiped themselves out almost to the man, the handful left petitioned other clans for membership. The Tefize were dumb enough to take Lirory."

"And he took over," finished Lan.

"Hard to believe a bunch of shit-movers would even think about having a sneaky mage in their ranks, and now they've got one running their clan business."

It was always this way, Lan mused. A powerful enough sorcerer had advantages over everyone else. Mostly the mages were reclusive and desired nothing but their own solitude. Occasionally, with ones like Claybore and this Lirory Tefize, they nurtured ambitions spanning worlds. They were the dangerous ones. They were the ones Lan had to fight.

"I sense Lirory," he said. "And Claybore. He shines like a black flame. But there is another presence, one I can't penetrate."

"Those are the real corpse-makers around here," said Broit. "The pair of them keeps us dragging, it does."

"Lan?" came a soft voice. "Are you all right?"

"Are you?" he asked Inyx.

"If we're inside the mountain and together, the answer's 'yes.'"

"I must have alerted Claybore to our presence," he told her. "The air elemental was like a finger pointing us out to him."

"We survived the fog. We can survive Claybore."

"I hope so, but there are things within this mountain I don't understand." He told her of Lirory Tefize and the powerful emanations he felt from the gnome clan leader and of the undecipherable radiations from still another mage. "Worst of all, I feel a very strong force within Yerrary. Claybore might be able to recover more than just one bodily part."

"How many are here?" she asked.

"Four. They might be his arms and legs."

"Why are all four here?"

"Lirory," broke in Broit Heresler. "He walks the Road and he's been collecting dead parts from all over. Why, nobody can say. We wanted to bury them, but he got huffy about it."

"Lirory's been accumulating them. For Claybore? Or for his own ends?"

"Any Tefize is a slippery character," said Broit. "Who can say?"

"He might be bartering the parts for concessions from Claybore," said Inyx. "Such a trade would appeal to Claybore. He wouldn't have to scour the worlds on his own to regain much of his power."

"Broit said there weren't any grey-clads on this world. This might be because of Lirory Tefize. He holds Claybore's legions at bay with the threat of destroying the body parts he controls."

"Claybore would make him ruler of the entire planet if he turned over the parts," said Inyx. "Why hasn't he already done so?"

"Lirory is ambitious. He holds out for more, if I know that bugger," said Broit.

"What more can there be?" asked Krek, finally shaking off his depression. "A world? A hundred worlds? What price is too high for Claybore to pay?"

Lan thought it over and finally said, "I don't know, but it might have something to do with the other presence I feel. Potent magics not of Claybore's doing are present. Perhaps Lirory bargains with two parties."

"Another Claybore?" groaned Krek. "Is not one ample for our feeble efforts?"

"I don't know what's going on. We'll have to check it out personally and see. Broit, lead on."

"You certain you want to ally with the Heresler?" the gnome asked. "These other clans have some high-class talent aiding them, damn them all. So why us?"

"We like you," said Inyx, laying her hand on the gnome's shoulder. Broit looked confused. Perhaps it was the first time anyone had ever told him he was likable.

"I only asked because it's taken us so long getting inside. We're going to have to cross Nichi territory to get safe."

"Who are they?"

"Sweepers," the gnome said with some disgust. "All they

do is push their filthy brooms around the corridors, stirring up dust and dissension. Awful people. And ugly! They are enough to make you die just looking at them."

Lan said nothing. Broit Heresler hardly appeared to be the height of beauty, but different worlds had different standards. He looked at Krek and had to smile. The spider always chided him on not having enough legs. And Krek's bride Klawn—Lan had seen her. The spider's description of her hardly jibed with reality. Larger even than Krek, she had tried to devour him on their wedding night and still Krek described her as loving and petite and the epitome of spiderish pulchritude.

"Are you going to take root or come along?" Broit asked snappishly.

"You lead, we follow. I'll keep a lookout for Claybore."

Inyx shot Lan a quick, anxious look and he shook his head to reassure her that Claybore was not near.

"This is a claustrophobic place," muttered Krek. "Look at the terribly constricted halls. Not like a good web spun across a mountain valley. Imagine living inside the mountain, rather than dangling from the outer slopes."

"Remember the rain and the fog," said Inyx. "And you saw how the rock burned when the rain hit it. Would you want a web exposed to those conditions?"

"It is as I said. This is a terrible place. Friend Lan Martak, let us hasten off this world and onto another, more bucolic one."

"We've work to do here, Krek. But don't worry. I don't want to stay here any more than you do."

"What's wrong with Home?" shouted Broit Heresler. "Isn't this good enough for you buggers? Looks great to me. Fine place. Fine."

"I'm sure," said Inyx, trying to soothe the gnome's anger, "Yerrary will grow on us."

"You make it sound like a fungus. This is a great place to live. Wait 'til you see our clan territory. Best in all of the mountain. You'll like it—you'll see."

Lan held up his hand cautioning Inyx and Krek. His light mote familiar bobbed about and returned. On its rippling surface he "read" what lay ahead of them in the hewn-rock tunnel.

For almost a hundred yards there were no cross-corridors. The rock itself was firm and virtually impenetrable, the tunnel being lit by phosphorescent moss growing on the roof and walls, casting a glow in such a way that there were no shadows anywhere. This all-pervading light erased shadows caused by contours and gave an odd appearance to both clothing and people. But beyond that was a chamber holding no fewer than twenty gnomes.

"Broit, is this way safe? There are many of your people ahead and waiting." Lan couldn't interpret whether or not those ahead were of the Heresler clan or another. From all Broit had said, he doubted they were friendly.

"It had better be safe. It's the only way back to Heresler territory without leaving Yerrary and daring the slopes." The gnome shivered with disgust at the idea of braving the elements outside his precious Home once more.

"Behind us is nothing," said Lan. "Shall we go forward?" He glanced from Inyx to Krek. Both nodded, knowing he would not lightly ask this question.

Broit already stormed ahead, swinging his short arms and leaning forward as he walked.

"The moss tickles," complained Krek. The giant spider brushed the top of his body along the tunnel roof as he went. "And it tastes awful." He made a spitting noise.

"Nichi!" cried Broit. "Those are the sweepers and they're waiting for us!"

"I told you," said Lan. He conjured a small spell to brush the gnomes from their path, then felt the spell snuffed out like a candle in a hurricane. "We are under attack magically," he said.

Inyx and Krek found themselves already occupied with

swarming gnomes taking swings at them with brooms and rakes. Broit Heresler shrieked and cavorted about, kicking and gouging and biting. All in all, this part of the battle appeared ineffectual.

Lan Martak felt the magics building around him, powerful magics able to smash cities, to wreck entire worlds. This was the real battle. Lose it and he lost all.

CHAPTER FOUR

Lan Martak sidestepped a broom handle thrust for his mid-section. He hardly noticed the rake that began its descent, aimed squarely for the top of his head. Inyx fielded that one, her steel sword blade deflecting the blow that wouldn't have greatly injured Lan but would have distracted him from his conjurings.

That break in his concentration might have proven fatal.

Coming toward them, channeled by the walls of the tunnel was *something*. Lan tried to put words to describing it and failed. The creature writhed and twisted and cavorted—and spewed forth noxious gases that made only those not of the Nichi clan gasp and wheeze.

"Magics," he said.

"Awful," said Krek. "It is starting to cause my fur to bristle and fall out in huge clumps. Absolutely awful."

Lan had to smile. Krek vowed that the human sense of smell was only a wild tale concocted to make him feel inferior. The spider's sense of taste amounted to little more than differentiating between dry and succulent, but his other

43

senses were acute in the extreme, especially his ability to sense vibration.

"Feel anything moving? Or is this pure illusion?" Lan asked the arachnid.

Krek drove talons into the rock walls and floor and stood for a moment, as if considering a weighty problem. Finally satisfied, he withdrew and said, "Nothing material comes."

Lan nodded and turned his full attention to the inexorably moving monster blocking their path in the tunnel. He ignored the fight between the gnomes and Inyx; her prowess far exceeded theirs. They danced in and out, poking and swinging their brooms, but they feared her flashing sword and quick, deadly lunges.

Lan muttered a small spell, then wove a blazing pattern in the air before him. The pattern shifted, burnt out, then exploded silently, ashes scattering out and over the groping apparition almost atop them.

The ashes lightly fluttered down and brushed the creature's leather hide. It shivered, then gave voice to a heart-rending shriek of the purest agony. With a puff of smoke, it vanished, leaving behind only the telltale fumes it had emitted on its track down the corridor.

"What of them?" asked Krek, pointing to the gnomes still tentatively battling Inyx. "Shall I eat them?"

"No!" cried Broit Heresler. "You can't do that. It's against the law."

"These Nichi clansmen want to kill you, don't they? Haven't they aligned themselves with the Tefize?" Lan puzzled over the gnome's insistence on not harming those attacking.

"Of course they have. Dismember them, torture them, do as you will. Kill them by all means. But don't eat them! There wouldn't be a fit corpse left to bury!"

Krek snorted in derision and plopped himself down to watch the gnomes and humans come to terms. Some forms of combat he simply did not understand and never would.

Lan almost shared his friend's opinion this time.

"You have to be able to bury the corpse for religious reasons?" he asked. Inyx still held at bay the entire pack of Nichi clan sweepers. He saw no great need for haste in this matter. The magical creature had been banished back to the limbo from which it had been conjured and the gnomes were ineffectual fighters at best.

"Yerrary take us, no! If you eat the damn bodies, there won't be any work for the Heresler. We're gravediggers. Damn fine ones, too. We have to protect our jobs, though. And from the likes of *him*. Who'd have thought it?" Broit Heresler jerked his thumb in Krek's direction. The spider impassively watched.

"So you don't care if I do this?" Lan moved so that he spun in a small circle, his arm waving free. As the tip of his index finger passed the position of each Nichi, they gasped and fell heavily to the floor. The harder they tried to stand, the worse their condition became. "The spell is simple enough. It confuses their limbs, weakens them, and increases the debility the more they struggle."

"Can't bury 'em 'til they're dead," complained Broit.

"That's not our worry," said Lan.

"Well," Broit said, "maybe we can bend the rules. If nobody's watching, you know?"

Inyx came over and sheathed her sword when she saw what Lan had done to the gnomes.

"How long will they be like that?" she asked.

"Can't say. This is the first time I've ever tried the spell. I don't believe it's permanent. It's too weak a spell."

"Effective. You ought to have tried it sooner. We could have used it any number of times."

"The spell seems to have come along with the tongue. I...I can't quite explain how or why. There are simply things popping up in my mmeory that were never there before. Spells, vague remembrances of other places and people."

"We'd best continue on. This little reception party might only be the start. And whoever sent the magical creature intended us real harm." Inyx skirted the edge of the group of kicking, complaining gnomes and entered the corridor beyond. "This is the way, isn't it, Broit?"

"Yes, of course it is," the diminutive gravedigger said. "Heresler territory is only a ways beyond."

Lan trailed the others, unsure about their safety. The creature he had vanquished had been too easily destroyed. And it had not been sent by Claybore. The "feel" of the dismembered sorcerer was not contained within the structure of the monster.

"Ahead," came Krek's warning, "lies a tunnel filled with more of the gnomes. They tap their feet and anxiously scrape the sides of the tunnel. I believe this means they will attack when we get near enough."

"Oh, no!" moaned Broit Heresler. "This is the Nichi's favorite ambush spot. We can't go back, either. A tunnel curves around. By the time we retreated, they'd be there to cut us off. We've got to fight because we can't run. No way."

"Some guide you are," muttered Inyx. "You lead us right into the middle of the enemy."

"Listen, skyscraper," Broit said, coming up to Inyx, tipping his head back and peering straight up into her face, "this part of Yerrary is pretty simple, but it's not Heresler territory. We don't have a lot of different ways we can go."

"Do the Nichi often attack?" asked Krek.

"Not too often," Broit said. "Today they are. Our bad luck. I only hope one of the really good diggers gets my body. Hate to be laid away in a slipshod grave."

"We wouldn't want that, now would we?" said Inyx with sugary sweetness.

"Don't need to be sarcastic," Broit muttered, lowering his eyes to the floor and shuffling his feet a little.

"Lan?" called back Inyx. "What do we do? What do you see?"

"Magic is all around. Claybore is near. He does nothing to aid the attack. He's not even aware of it, but the other mage is."

"What other mage?"

"I don't know. But Claybore...digs. He's excavating to find something. Huge amounts of power emanate from that pit."

"Another part of his body?" asked Inyx.

"It must be more than a single part. Not even the tongue radiated this particular type of aura, and it carried with its spells of immense power."

"Where?" asked Krek. "I feel the gnomes ahead. Where is Claybore?"

Lan pointed without seeing. His finger directed their attention through solid rock. Krek and Inyx exchanged looks and shook their heads. This was a seeing beyond simple vision.

"We can't go after Claybore and fight off the Nichi. Not if what Broit says is true," said Inyx.

"Are you calling me a liar, skyscraper?" demanded Broit.

"Nothing of the sort," said Inyx. "We're just trying to sort out what our best course of action is."

"Use the funny tanglefoot spell again. That'll stop them all," said Broit. "I liked watching those Nichi flopping about as if they'd just fallen out of the stewpot."

"It will also alert Claybore. The numbers of Nichi this time are a score more than we encountered the first time. And he is so close. So very close." Lan's voice trailed off as he "watched" the excavation proceeding. Claybore did not detect him because the mage's full attention was directed to whatever was within the pit.

"Ahead, then to the right," said Lan. "That is the best way to approach Claybore. I can attack him directly when I can see him."

"Aren't you seeing him now?" asked Broit. "What's with you, man? You talk in riddles."

"He is a mage," said Krek. "Not that good a one, at

times, but still, a mage. We all know they are a bit off in the head."

"Oh, yeah, righto."

"The next intersection," said Lan, almost in a dreamlike state of concentration now. "We go right and then I'll be able to see him directly, with my own eyes. The attack. How do I attack?"

"That intersection's where the Nichi will clobber us," said Broit. "Their favorite spot for ambush, it is. Yes, indeed."

"Broit, does Heresler territory lie directly down this corridor?"

"Not more than a mile further down. No turnings, just a straight-ahead run."

"Then," said Inyx grimly, "we will run the entire way. You first. I'll follow and make sure they come for us." Her sword slipped easily from its sheath. This time she knew she'd spill blood with it. The woman almost thrilled to that. She was a warrior and enjoyed a good battle. The way Lan now fought with spells and geases and creatures that weren't quite real did not appeal to her. Such magics had their place, but would never replace a well-fought duel with swords— or hand to hand.

"Let me make sure this is the way you want it," said Broit. The gnome uneasily wiped perspiration from his wrinkled forehead, chunks of dirt falling away. "I run through the junction and get them chasing me. You come after, hacking and slashing at them before they catch up with me? What then?"

"The others follow me," said Inyx.

"What about them?" Broit looked suspiciously at Krek and Lan.

"They take the right tunnel and find Claybore."

"Why not let the spider come with us? He, uh, he'd make a good decoy. Better than me."

"He goes with Lan," Inyx said firmly. She wanted Lan

to have some physical protection along the way. While the man was an expert swordsman, the conjurings took too much of his attention. Krek could fend off any attack until Lan's defenses were properly formed—and the battle taken to Claybore.

"Let him use just a *little* spell on the Nichi," begged Broit. "That'll take some of the pressure off you."

"We do it this way. If Lan casts too potent a spell, he'd draw Claybore's attention. That would be the end for all of us."

"If I attack first, when he is not prepared, this might end it. The contest would be over once and for all," Lan said, more to himself than to the others. It seemed too incredible to believe, all the agony, all the death and destruction behind them. Victory would be his with a single magical bolt.

"Let's gooooo!" cried Inyx, running off and prodding Broit ahead of her with the naked edge of her sword. The gnome yelped and danced and ran like all the demons of the Lower Places chased after him. The gnome realized he might be better off if they were, too. Inyx brooked no small hesitation and gave freely of the flat of her sword, promising even more if Broit Heresler so much as thought of slowing his breakneck pace.

"They enter the intersection," said Krek. "The Nichi swarm out and follow Broit. Inyx follows this group. Ah, she has removed four of them from the fracas. Such expertise with her weapon. A pity she is human. What a fine spider she would have made. Not as good as my Klawn, of course; but still, a fine arachnid."

"Now," said Lan, almost in a trance. "We must go now. Hurry. Claybore is nearing the end of the excavation. He is close to retrieving whatever lies in the pit."

The intersection was devoid of life. Several gnome corpses lay strewn about where Inyx's deadly blade had separated them from their lives. From further down the corridor came sounds of a fierce battle raging. Shouts, screams of agony, the shuffle of feet, and the clank of metal weapons. These Nichi were armed with more than brooms.

"Inyx makes the battle sound interesting," said Krek, his huge body swaying toward that corridor, and then in the direction where Claybore worked so feverishly to retrieve still another bodily part.

"If I attack without hesitation, I can end it all," said Lan. "I will! This is it, Krek. We'll be victorious. I know it!"

Lan ran off, Krek trailing behind. The spider's pace became slower and slower as they went, because of the narrowing tunnel. He soon scooted along, legs bent almost double. Mumbling about the idiocy of this quest, the spider eventually came into a small antechamber. Lan stood, his face turned toward a dark opening in the wall before them.

"Claybore is through there," he said. Lan quaked inside, but it was not with fear. This was the shivering of anticipation, of need to begin. He had met Claybore in magical battle before. Neither had been able to vanquish the other. But now, with Claybore's tongue resting within his mouth, Lan Martak knew he had the power and the ability to stop the sorcerer.

"Let us not keep him waiting," said Krek. "I want to return to the peaks of my beloved el-Liot Mountains and once more feel the wind whispering seductively through my leg fur." He rubbed one thick foreleg against another and saw even larger patches fall off. Krek sniffed indignantly at this. "Let us definitely put an end to all this chasing about."

Lan Martak stormed forward, his spells already forming on his lips. His dancing light mote familiar raced to his aid, built the power about him, built into a spear of pure magic, and turned until it aimed directly at Claybore.

The sorcerer's mechanical legs remained firmly planted, but the upper torso spun so that the fleshless skull peered directly at Lan.

"You!" came the soundless cry. In the pits of those dark eye sockets came a stirring, a beginning of the ruby death beams.

With a single gesture, Lan snuffed out those death beacons. His triumph towered and he released the bolt of pure magic.

Claybore let out a shriek of total agony. Never before had Lan been able to carry the battle to Claybore. With the tongue, Lan Martak was more than a match for the disembodied sorcerer. His power surging, Lan launched a new and different form of attack. Again came Claybore's immediate anguish.

"Stop," the sorcerer begged. "We can rule together. Stop this!" He tried to mount a counteroffensive. Lan crushed the attack before it had even halfway formed to menace him.

"You have created untold misery along the Road," said Lan. "Your mindless rush to regain that stripped from you by Terrill is now at an end. Terrill was unable to destroy you. I might be unable, also. But I *feel* it within my power. Using your own tongue against you, using the spells locked forever with it, using the grimoire I obtained atop Mt. Tartanius from another of your foes, I can destroy you."

"No, stop. Please. We can negotiate."

In that instant Lan knew he had won. He formed another bolt and sent it directly for the center of Claybore's skull. The bone chipped and began cracking. Another bolt sailed for the Kinetic Sphere buried within Claybore's chest cavity. The pinkly pulsating sphere allowed the mage to move from one world to the next without using the cenotaphs. Lan wrapped the Kinetic Sphere in a layer of heavy spells that prevented Claybore from escaping.

Lan Martak formed the ultimate stroke. This carried the full force of every spell he commanded, used the full resources he had gained along the Cenotaph Road.

Claybore stood helpless before him.

The spell was cast—cast and deflected at the last possible instant. Lan blinked in surprise. This could not have happened, yet it did. Claybore lacked the necessary power to save himself.

"Lirory!" cried the dismembered sorcerer. "Aid me now! Again! Aid me again!"

Standing with hands folded at the far side of the pit was a gnome. His eyes blazed emerald green and brighter than any sun.

"This must be the wizard of the Tefize clan Broit spoke of," said Krek.

The spider spat forth a hunting web, intending to tangle the gnome and pull him into the pit. The web vaporized inches before striking the sorcerer gnome.

"I am no novice," said Lirory Tefize.

"Aid me, Tefize!" pleaded Claybore.

"The arms can be yours—in exchange for that which we have mentioned," bargained the gnome.

"Yes, yes! He kills me!"

"An immortal dying? How terrible," said Lirory Tefize, mocking Claybore. "That is unthinkable." The gnome's entire stature altered, grew. Power blasted from his thick body until Lan had to throw up hands to shield his eyes. He recovered and caught up his familiar light mote, using it to absorb some of this prodigious energy.

Lan knew the tide of battle had turned against him. Unless he quickly summoned all his magical lore, he would die, and Krek and Inyx and untold millions of others would spend their lives under the yoke of tyranny Claybore promised.

He had summoned the ebon dragon once. He did so again. The huge creature filled the room, its nothingness reaching out and taking all the punishment Lirory Tefize and Claybore could offer. It sucked in their energies and demanded more. Lan urged it forward, to attack, to absorb the sorcerers as it now sucked at their power.

"An unusual manifestation," said the gnome. "Can you see it, mage? Allow me to show it to you."

Lan screamed. Somehow, the emptiness of the dragon was pulled inside out and revealed fully to him. He saw death and misery of every conceivable form. It gnawed at his mind, jerked at his emotions, tore him away from the battle.

Again the protective light mote saved him. As Lan cowered from the horrors revealed within his dragon, Claybore attacked. The savage lunge of pure energy sank into the light mote and—almost—penetrated through to the other side. How a single point of light had dimension Lan didn't know or even want to consider now. That it had thwarted still another of Claybore's assaults was sufficient.

"The pit widens," said Krek. The spider stepped back, but the edge followed him. He and Lan were soon trapped on a single ledge, their backs to the stone wall of Yerrary.

"It works in other ways," said Lan, regaining his composure. He had panicked for a moment when Tefize joined the battle. Fighting two mages might be difficult, but it wasn't impossible. Not for him!

Krek started to say something, when he noticed what Lan did. The very rock melted and flowed all around. Tefize and Claybore found their footing increasingly vitreous. Tefize sank to his knees, his waist. Claybore's mechanical legs were entirely drawn down into the rock.

"Freeze!" cried Lan, sending forth a wave of intense cold. The molten rock returned to its normal solidity, now holding both sorcerers firmly in its grasp.

"That ought to hold them," said Krek. But the spider worried. He shot forth web after web, trying to stick it to the ceiling and swing over to the encapsulated mages. Lirory Tefize vaporized every single strand as it flew toward the ceiling.

"I know, Krek," comforted Lan. "The pair of them work well together. I shall have to do something more, it seems."

He and Krek had been trapped on a ledge along the pit. Now the ledge grew, flowed and merged with solider portions of the cave floor. Soon enough they were on firm footing again and no longer threatened with a long fall into the excavation.

"You have beaten me, Lan Martak," said Claybore without a hint of rancor. This more than anything else put Lan on guard. Claybore would never surrender. Not this easily. Not when there was a single spell yet to be cast, a single geas to be applied.

"Then I want proof of it!" shouted Lan. He blasted outward with the most devastating spell of which he was capable. Lan almost laughed aloud when he saw Claybore's skull begin to split in half.

Then he screamed. From within the skull came insects of all sizes and shapes. Pincers snapping, mosquito-stingers probing, the cloud of insects erupted forth and filled the entire chamber.

Spell after spell failed. Lan used the Voice to make the insects disperse. Nothing happened. Krek attempted to eat them. He spat out the hideous creatures and silently offered his apology to Lan.

From every side the insects came at him—and Tefize and Claybore added magical jabs until he fought simply to remain sane. His body slowly being gnawed away by the bugs, his mind railing against the renewed assault by the two sorcerers, his emotions torn between admitting he had failed and retreating or staying and fighting to the death, Lan Martak was gradually beaten back.

"Friend Lan Martak, let us leave immediately," urged the spider. "We have lost this bout. There will be another."

"Go, Krek," sobbed out Lan. "You go. Whatever they've done to me, I can't move. My legs are numb."

"The insects do their work well," said Lirory Tefize with some satisfaction.

"I give you my sincerest congratulations. I had not thought this ploy would work," said Claybore. "But it has!"

Lan Martak was beaten ever backward by the opposing magics and his body was being devoured by the insects. Truly, he had now lost both battle and war.

CHAPTER FIVE

"Look out!" cried Inyx, lunging to prevent the wooden stick from landing squarely atop Broit Heresler's pointed head. The gnome didn't even take note of her quick action. He snorted and kicked and kept fighting. But Inyx saw the tide of battle inexorably going against them. While it was noble of her to provide a decoy for Lan and Krek to find and fight Claybore, she wasn't about to die under a wave of gnomes brandishing sticks and brooms and the occasional knife and spear.

"Let's get out of here," she said to Broit. "We can take that passage and cut down the number of them following us."

"The Nichi know all these tunnels," complained the gnome. "I don't. If only we could reach Heresler territory. *Then* things would be different. We'd have them turned into corpses in nothing flat."

Inyx didn't have the wind to tell Broit that escape was more important than making the most number of dead bodies. She didn't want to stand and fight; she wanted to flee and find a quiet spot to recuperate. Her body was covered with growing black-and-blue spots and one throbbing bruise over her right knee caused her to limp slightly. She doubted the bone had been injured when the Nichi fighter had smashed her with the rock, but only a closer examination would tell for certain.

Right now, she fought mostly on adrenaline.

"We can't run. It's not sporting," said Broit.

"We can't stay and let them pick us off. We're only two against their many."

"A Heresler fights."

"You can damned well die a Heresler, then!" snapped Inyx. She slashed and hacked her way through a small knot of gnomes and fought into the corridor, stumbling when her right leg gave way under her. She rolled, came to her feet, and braced herself for a moment against the rock wall.

To her surprise, a gnarly arm supported her until she got her leg moving properly.

"Thanks, Broit. I thought you were staying to fight."

"Let's run. We can discuss this matter elsewhere."

"In Heresler territory?"

"Certainly."

The pair of them ran, Broit's short legs doing a good job of keeping up with Inyx's longer-legged strides. But run as they would, the Nichi followed, screaming their vengeance as they came. The dark-haired woman wondered what drove those gnomes. Many of them lay dead and more than a score had acquired nasty-looking wounds. If they broke off the attack, they could claim a victory.

But the Nichi attacked and attacked and attacked.

Inyx fought, turned down different corridors, fought some more, doubled back, and eventually got herself lost in the rocky maze that was Yerrary.

By the time she lunged, spitted the gnome confronting her, and watched the misshapen creature buckle and fall dead, Inyx realized she and Broit Heresler had become

separated. She couldn't even remember the exact moment—
or the exact place.

"This doesn't look too promising," she said aloud. In
every direction she turned, the tunnels appeared the same.
Grey rock with the clinging phosphorescent moss on the
ceilings and no sign of life or shadow. "Where do I go
now?"

Inyx tried to backtrack by following the faint evidence
of scuffle marks on the floor, but this took her in circles.
The woman tried cutting small blazes into the stone wall to
show her route and quickly discovered herself even more
lost in the tunnels.

Closing her eyes, she concentrated on Lan Martak. Recently, they had forged a mind to mind link that both thrilled
and frightened her. Never had she been so close to any man
than when she and Lan made love and the mental link formed
along with the physical.

But it was closed to her.

"And why not?" she said to herself, more for the com-
forting sound of her words than any other reason. "He's
battling Claybore. He has no time for linking with me." She
shuddered at the prospect of disturbing Lan at the wrong
instant. Such would cause him great danger. Inyx almost
felt guilty at the attempt, even though she desperately needed
to know how to find her way through this confusing maze.

"I've been in worse." She harkened back to the time
spent in the Twistings, a prison filled with sudden death
and prisoners both human and inhuman. Inyx had survived
that and thwarted Claybore. She could do it again.

"After all," the woman said, brightening, "this maze
doesn't have the monsters in it that the Lord of the Twistings
put in his. This is home to a huge number of gnomes. They'd
remove any monsters out of self-defense." She worried over
that for a moment, then added, "Broit Heresler would certainly do that. If only to bury the bodies."

Laughing, she set off in a random direction. At one cross-tunnel, a faint breeze blew across her perspiring face. She turned and walked into it, hoping to find an entrance populated with people she could ask for directions.

The woman stopped dead in her tracks when she saw the aqueduct. Coming through a huge hole in the side of the mountain, the waterway filled with rain and spiraled the water to lower levels in Yerrary. She swallowed hard when she saw that the water set the ductways afire. The acid rain had the same effect on this artificial creation as it did on the natural plains outside Yerrary.

"What do they drink here?" she wondered. Such water would sear and burn away anyone's innards. Inyx felt her throat tightening as she tried to remember when last she'd had a drink of water. The battles had caused her to sweat freely and she had been on another world when last she'd eaten.

Inyx walked forward until she stood only a few feet from the trough of burning water. Looking upward through the tiny entrance, she saw the leaden sky outside. The fiery rains continued to pelt down their acid punishment and what little she saw of the mountainside burned in tiny, maniacally dancing watchfires. The ductway itself was filled to the rim with the acid water.

Dropping to her knees, she peered down, trying to see where the water exited the system. Level after level below Inyx saw, until darkness robbed her of any idea exactly how deep the aqueduct went. She saw a full five hundred feet and there was no end in sight at that point.

"The mountain is the highest thing to be seen on this world and the gnomes have hollowed out the world all the way to the core." She shook her head in amazement.

Slinging her sword over her shoulder and onto her back, she edged over to the ductway and carefully swung down. The water splashed onto her fingers and burned, but not to the point of real pain. She knew she could stand the acid's action for a while before flesh began to peel away. Still,

Inyx felt the need to hurry her explorations.

Hand over hand she went down the spiraling aqueduct until she came to the next level. More tunnels. There was nothing to differentiate these from those above.

Down to the next level and the next and the next. All the same, until she came to the seventh level below her starting point. On impulse she walked through the tunnels for a short distance, then stopped and simply stared at the wall and wanted to cry.

"My mark!" she wailed. Scratched at her eye level was one of the first cuts she'd made in the stone to give her some idea as to direction in Yerrary. Somehow she had managed to go up all those levels in her wanderings and not even know it.

Then she brightened a little. She stood a much better chance of finding Lan and Krek if she stayed here than blundering about up where she had been.

"Then again, I might explore a lower level, then return here. It wouldn't be so hard." She returned to the aqueduct of fire and lowered herself one more level. Inyx was glad she had done this, because it satisfied some of her curiosity about the gnomes' arrangements for drinking water.

The acid rainwater came to a halt at this level by pouring into a giant vat that steamed and smoked. Looking at it dissuaded her from wanting to take a quick swim. The very flesh would be stripped off her body in seconds if she immersed herself in that water. But the water itself ran from the vat into a tangle of lead pipes and from there into glass distillation units.

She explored, but found no one around. Everything appeared to be fully mechanized and didn't require constant attention. She toyed with the idea of turning off the water and seeing who would come to fix the problem—or if anyone at all would come. The gnomish clans had their society's jobs segmented and some clans apparently were more diligent than others about performing their tasks. Perhaps whatever clan ran the stills had simply left to go about other more entertaining activities.

She came to another vat, this one filled with crystal clear water. Hesitantly Inyx stuck her finger into the water. No burning. Nothing. Her thirst assailed her more than ever. Inyx had to make the effort. Cupping her hand, she pulled forth enough for a taste. While the water had a curiously flat taste to it, no burning sensation accompanied the coolness laving her tongue or running down her throat.

"Water. Drinkable water," she said with some satisfaction.

As she leaned forward to truly drink, a voice snapped out at her, "You're not allowed to drink. Only the Wartton clan is allowed to decant from that vat."

She jerked erect, hand on sword. Inyx's bright blue eyes slowly scanned the dimness of the distillation room. She saw no one.

"Mind's playing tricks on me," she said aloud, hoping the words would soothe her. Instead, it provoked an answer from her unseen watcher.

"That may be, but you are not allowed to drink from that vat. Only the Wartton are allowed. Please leave."

"Who are you?" she demanded. "Where are you?"

"Please don't make me get tough. I don't like beating up on people. But I will if I have to!"

The way the words were spoken, the tone, the quavering inflections told Inyx a different story. Whoever spoke not only didn't like fighting, he had never done it at all.

"Join me in robbery, then," she said. She drank deeply of the water until she had her fill. All the while the voice blustered and threatened ineffectually.

"How dare you! I shall have to report this immediately!"

"Do as you like," Inyx said. "But we can talk this out if you'll show yourself. I won't hurt you. I promise that much."

"Will you take more of the water?"

"I might."

"But you won't hurt me? And you won't tell the Warttons what you've done?"

"No, I won't," she said, laughing.

From the shadows of another vat scuttled a brown toad-like creature with a wattle bobbing nervously under its bony chin. Saucer-huge eyes peered at Inyx, trying to evaluate how much she had lied about not wanting to harm it.

"Come along," she said. "Let's sit and talk." On a level with the creature, she saw it was even more offensive looking and even more harmless than she'd thought on first glance. Tiny fingers nervously twined and untwined and a long tongue flickered out and back as if snaring insects from midair.

"Who are you?" the creature demanded, trying to draw itself up to match Inyx.

"I'm a traveler along the Cenotaph Road. Friends of mine and I entered Yerrary and became separated from our guide, Broit Heresler. Do you know him?"

"Broit? Well, he's all right, I suppose. Bossy. He thinks he ought to be the head of the Heresler clan."

"He is now. The former clan leader, uh, met with an accident out on the plains."

"Oh."

Inyx frowned. Getting information from this little beast might prove impossible. It didn't appear too intelligent.

"I'm Eckalt," it said finally.

"Your name or position?"

"My name, of course. My position is obvious. I am director of the distillery."

"All this is yours?" Inyx asked in surprise.

"I built it all. I told those awful gnomes how to get real water from the acid. And how do they treat me? Terribly, that's how. Without me, they'd die. As it is, they let me distill their water and give me supplies enough to survive. I do have a quite nice pond in the back."

"I'm sure it has lily pads and everything."

"What are lilies?" Eckalt demanded. "Is there another who gets these lilies when I don't? How dare they! The gnomes misuse me horribly!"

"Why don't you leave?"

"Where would I go? Yerrary is my home, too, as much as it belongs to them."

"If they aren't treating you as you'd like, stand up for your rights. Surely, someone as important as you are to the gnomes should be accorded some respect."

"I have a plan," the toadlike being said, rubbing his hands together in a conspiratorial fashion. "I know how to get even with them all. And I'll do it, too!"

"You're going to poison the water?"

"Who told you? Who told you?" The creature bounced around on oversized hind legs until Inyx thought he'd jump into a vat of his own water. Then pure panic seized him and he cowered away from her. "You're a spy. The gnomes sent you to spy on me, to find out my plans. How'd you do it? I demand to know!"

"I'm no spy. It only makes sense that the easiest way of retaliating would be for you to do something to the water. If they rely on you, then you control them. Destroy the water supply and they have to do as you say if they want it built up again."

"They'd never go along with that," the creature said dubiously.

"Have you tried it?"

"Well, no."

"They have sorcerers, don't they? How likely would a sorcerer be to come down here and dirty his hands with all this plumbing?"

"The Tefize sorcerer is one of the last. All the others got made into corpses. The Hereslers enjoyed that, I'm sure. But Lirory, he'd never even think of it. Sooner would he send some minion out onto the plains to find the naturally occurring pure waters."

"The sweepers?" Inyx pressed on. "Would they do anything to you?"

"They can't even keep the corridors clean."

"The Heresler?"

"All they do is dig graves and drag bodies about. Frightful people. And they smell bad, too."

"Who else?" Inyx pressed. "Is there any group who could duplicate all you've done here?"

"Not in Yerrary."

"See?" The woman didn't know why she was bothering with the timid little creature. She knew he would never do any of the things he plotted. Still, it intrigued her that such a being proved to be the mastermind that kept a vital part of Yerrary functioning.

And, she had to admit, she had taken a liking to him.

"But there's another who would make me do it."

"Who?" The way Eckalt spoke of this other person caught her attention. Awe and fear intermixed in a way different from the toad-being's talk of the gnomes.

"The Resident of the Pit."

Inyx sat and stared at Eckalt, wondering if the creature made this up. She had heard Lan's stories of his home world and of how the Resident of the Pit had persuaded him his only escape lay along the Road. It could be no more than coincidence if two beings used the same title.

"He is all-powerful, but he is like I am. He never does anything. He sits and waits and watches. Like I do. He says he is an elder god whose time is past. I don't believe him. He . . . he waits for something. I model myself after him and his patience. My time will come, too. Wait and see!"

"I'm sure it will, Eckalt. Where is this Resident of the Pit?"

The toad creature made a vague motion upward and said,

"Directions in Yerrary are so confusing. I find the pit now and again, more by chance than anything else. But he is around. He is always in the pit. I don't think he can leave."

Inyx decided the pit had to be somewhere near. She didn't think Eckalt was the type to go exploring as she'd done in her modest way. The creature probably traveled no more than a few hundred yards in any single direction from his distillation equipment before hopping back to his lilyless pond and cowering in fear the rest of the day.

"Do you know anything of Claybore?" she asked.

"The skeleton with the mechanical legs?"

"You do know of him," said Inyx. "Tell me all you can of him, Eckalt."

"He and the Tefize are in alliance. It is his assistant whom I dislike. An ugly woman, much like you."

Inyx decided not to take offense. Anyone Eckalt thought ugly might be considered comely by human standards. After all, Eckalt had wattles, was a dun color, and had warts discoloring his skin in a hundred spots. On top of that, he was more frog than human.

"Light brown hair, a certain feral look in her eye? Her name is Kiska k'Adesina?"

"Possibly. The physical description is close enough, but I've never heard a name."

"Why does she come here—to bother you?"

"Oh, does she ever bother me!" Eckalt exclaimed. "All the time badgering me about increasing supplies, cutting off water to some clans and aiding others. I tell her it is no good, that my system is perfect as it is. But she always makes suggestions—silly suggestions, too." Eckalt appeared indignant at such effrontery.

"Where can I find her?" asked Inyx as innocently as she could. The answer didn't please her.

Eckalt shrugged, his sloping shoulders hunching strangely.

Before Inyx said another word, the ring of metal on metal reached her ears. She froze. This was the familiar sound of battle and it came from the level just above this one—the one on which she thought she'd left Lan and Krek.

"How do I get up one level?" she asked.

"I do not know. There is a way," Eckalt began. "I think there is, at any rate. I seldom leave and..."

Inyx didn't stay to listen to the creature's further woes of not being adventurous. She raced back through the vats and lead piping and found the aqueduct. Flexing her muscles, she leaped, caught hold, and began inching her way back up the spiraling ductway. It took longer to reach the upper level than she'd thought; she feared the battle would be over and Lan would no longer need her assistance.

Inyx need not have worried about the struggle ending quickly. The woman pulled herself onto the level and traced her footsteps back to the spot where she'd blazed the mark on the wall. Not ten paces further down the corridor, she saw the broad back of a dark-headed man furiously lunging and swinging his sword. Every stroke severed fingers and hands and ears and still the gnomes rushed him.

Inyx let out a war whoop and drew her sword from over her shoulder. In her haste, the blade struck the ceiling. But this accident brought the fight to a momentary halt. Bright sparks leaped from the nicked edge of her blade and caught the attention of all those battling.

The gnomes muttered something about sorcery.

Inyx didn't give them the chance to think differently. They outnumbered the man forty to one. She vowed to cut down the odds from forty to two to even less.

Her first flèche skewered the lead gnome. He went down, air hissing obscenely from his punctured lungs.

"Nicely done," complimented the blood-soaked man to her right.

She blinked at him. He reminded her so of—but no, that wasn't possible. Her husband Reinhardt was long dead; she had held him in her arms and had buried him herself, a victim of Claybore's grey-clad legions. Only memories and magically induced visions of Reinhardt lingered to haunt her.

But the resemblance was still uncanny. This man had the same dark eyes, the same smile that curled sardonically at the corners of his lips, the straight nose and perfect bone structure. But there Inyx saw the similarity truly ended. This man was much more powerfully built. His wrist was half again the thickness of her dead husband's—and this man's skill with the blade surpassed even Reinhardt's.

"You've been doing a fair job yourself, good sir."

"Ducasien, my lady. My name is Ducasien."

"Inyx," she said.

"From Leponto Province?"

"You know my home?" She made a quick backhanded cut and heel-toe advanced cutting, slashing, thrusting. The Nichi clan gnome was no match with only a broom handle.

"I am from Leponto, myself."

"We must explore this further. When we have a spare moment!" Inyx began a serious attack and found herself coordinating smoothly with Ducasien. When she tired, he took up the fight. When his mighty thewed arms knotted from effort, she stood ready to join in, rested and ready for any number of attacking gnomes.

Before long even the Nichi clan recognized that the pair they fought were too skilled in combat. They broke off their attack and fled.

Panting, Inyx leaned on her blade and watched the tiny, hunched backs vanishing down the corridor.

"We put them to rout in good order," said Ducasien, laughing. Inyx felt shivers racing up and down her spine. When he spoke his voice came out as melodiously as Reinhardt's. The woman worried that Ducasien would prove another illusion, an hallucination conjured by her tired brain.

"Now that we have time," the man said, "let us compare lineages." He started in, detailing his ancestors and finishing with several of whom Inyx had never heard. She said as much.

"How long," Ducasien responded, "has it been since you were last home?"

"Time is fluid along the Road. Who can say? Perhaps five years is all it seems to me."

"It might be closer to fifty actual," said Ducasien. "My family moved only within the last twenty to Leponto. And I have walked the Road myself only for one year."

Inyx felt faint at the idea of being so totally cut off from her home world. Not only were her family and Reinhardt's dead, most of her onetime friends would be dead also. Even with Claybore's legions gone, there was little for her to return to in Leponto.

Ducasien read this sadness in her face.

"That is the price we pay for walking the Road. We trade security for adventure. But is it not worth the price?"

Inyx nodded, not trusting herself to speak. Again she was reminded of Reinhardt. Those were sentiments he might have uttered.

"I found this world by accident," Ducasien went on, filling the silence left by Inyx's thoughts. "Only a day or two has elapsed since I came here from a world almost totally covered with water. Finding the cenotaph on that world proved difficult. It was under water and guarded by the oddest of fish creatures."

"I've never heard of such a thing!" exclaimed Inyx, this piece of information bringing her out of her gloom. "We've never found such on any world we've traveled."

"We?"

"Lan Martak and Krek. The three of us have been together for some time." Inyx went on detailing their fight against Claybore.

"I knew the sorcerer was a threat, but I had no idea of the magnitude," said Ducasien when she had finished her story. "Do you need another sword to aid you? With this Martak being the mage you claim, a mere sword is hardly much to offer, but it is all I have. I fear I have never learned much of magics." His ebon-dark eyes locked with her bright blue ones. Again Inyx felt the shivers of memory, of old feelings stirring anew. She nervously broke eye contact and looked away.

"We should find them and give aid if we can," Ducasien went on. "Where are they?"

"I got lost. But it was on this level. Since my marks indicate I came from the other direction, they might be ahead."

"Those were your blaze marks? I had wondered. My sense of direction within the tunnels is rather good. Since I heard digging from that direction earlier in the day, let's try it first." Ducasien and Inyx went off, trading stories of home.

Only when Ducasien dropped into a defensive posture and whipped forth his sword did Inyx pay any attention to where they went.

"No!" she cried, gripping Ducasien's arm. "That's Krek. He's a friend."

"Some friend," muttered the man, easing out of his fighting position.

"Krek," Inyx said, going to where the spider huddled against one stone wall and openly wept. "What happened? Where's Lan?"

"Why am I always the one stepped on, always the one humiliated, always the one no one considers?" moaned the spider.

"What happened?" Inyx demanded, fear clutching her throat. "What happened to Lan? Did he stop Claybore?"

"Friend Inyx, even you ask after him. But he is no good."

"Lan? I don't understand. What went on?"

"Friend Lan Martak is my friend no more. He left me. He abandoned me without so much as a word, without even a backward look. To him I am nothing. Nothing! Oh, woe! Why did I ever leave my fine web?" The arachnid cried huge, salty tears now. They stained his coppery fur and he didn't even take notice.

Inyx realized then how serious the matter was.

She stood, the fear mounting inside to the point where she felt faint. Lan Martak had to be crazy to abandon a friend as staunch as Krek had been—or in the deepest trouble of his life.

CHAPTER SIX

Lan Martak sank to his knees on the narrow ledge, the snapping, stabbing, bloodsucking insects all around. The spells cast at him by Claybore and the gnome wizard Lirory Tefize further sapped his strength and his will to fight.

"You must not allow them to win so easily," said Krek.

"Easily!" cried Lan. "I fought. I . . . I can't fight any more."

"They do this to you. Their spells somehow rob you of all desire to continue. Protect yourself, friend Lan Martak. Protect yourself and do not think of me."

Lan glanced at the giant spider. Krek waved front legs back and forth in a futile attempt to ward off the insects. The swarming bugs bothered him as much as they did the human—and perhaps even more. They got into the coppery fur of his legs and burrowed, and then began sucking away at his life juices. Lan cried inside when he saw the sorry sight of Krek's blood dripping down those mighty legs.

Then he looked to his own body. The insects treated him

far worse. Not a square inch of exposed skin escaped unscathed. Fiery red marked where they chewed on him and their poisons entered his bloodstream, further debilitating him.

But worst of all by far was the spell cast upon him by Tefize.

The gnome slowly rose out of the rock into which Lan had cast him. The spell turning the stone into liquid had faded and Lan no longer maintained it, allowing Lirory Tefize to escape. And with him came Claybore. The mechanical legs had been damaged, bent and twisted into impossible shapes, but Claybore remained in full control of the powers he had recovered during their long battle along the Road.

The disembodied sorcerer used them all now.

Lan began to sob, to feel more and more insignificant. Why continue? The two mages' spells were too potent for him. He was only a simple hunter from a primitive world dabbling in the arcane. What did he know of magic? He was better off with sword in hand and even this ability had fled him. It had been far too long since he had relied on his strong arm and quick reflexes. What prowess with the blade he had once possessed was long past. He had gambled on attaining supreme magical power and had now lost that wager.

Lost. Lost. Lost!

"Lan," came Krek's soft voice. "The ledge narrows. They chew away at it even as their odious bugs chew at our flesh."

"What's the difference?" he moaned. "Let them cast us into the pit. It can't be any worse than this." His arms burned with the insects' poison and his brain was reduced to nothing more than lard renderings. Weak, incapable of forming a single thought, he felt he deserved to die.

Lan wiped sweat and blood from his eyes in time to see

Krek spit forth a web and swing upward. The spider worked quickly, easily, in spite of the injuries the swarming insects forced upon him. Lan knew he should take heart in this, but couldn't. He felt too miserable.

"Goodbye, Martak," came Claybore's gloating words. "Soon enough you will enjoy the fate I endured for so long. I shall rip the tongue from your mouth and regain it. And your body? That will be scattered along the Road as was mine. You will never die, but you will never again be alive, either."

The demonic laughter filled the chamber and reverberated down long corridors within the mountain.

And Lan sat with back against rock, feet dangling over the ledge and thought, really thought. The blackness at the edges of his brain lit up a little with the effort. His familiar dancing energy mote returned and cast light where only shadow had been. Lan Martak saw more clearly in that moment because of what Claybore had said.

Claybore was going to scatter his body along the Road? Lan Martak could never die? Could this be so? Had his magical powers grown to such a level that he and Claybore were alike in this respect?

"I cannot die?" he asked aloud.

From deep within his soul came a stirring, a feathery touch, a gentleness backed with seemingly infinite power. The answer formed and glowed within him like a beacon.

"No, you cannot die. You can oppose them. Do so. Now!"

"What? Who are you?" Lan cried. The sensation had been familiar and yet vastly different from any he had experienced before. He knew the words had been thrust into his head just as Claybore spoke, without physical words, but the feeling was entirely unlike the other mage's communication.

"You do not hallucinate. Fight Claybore. Fight Tefize.

Do it or you will suffer the fate Claybore has decreed for you."

"Help me!" Lan begged.

The power resided within him, but no further encouragement came. Lan again wiped blood from his eyes and peered aloft. Krek hung from a web, suspended over the pit. On the far side stood Claybore and Tefize. The gnome's entire body burned with an intensity that should have been painful to witness. Lan stared directly into the hot green blaze, into the twin orbs that matched the sun's intensity, and did so without flinching.

His familiar burst upon him now, ready to renew the battle.

"He fights well," commented Tefize in an offhand manner, "but he is weak. He will fail. Feel him slipping into depression once more?"

"Yes, Lirory. I feel it. So does he," answered Claybore.

But Lan felt only their redoubled efforts to cast their insidious spells. He rose and clapped his hands together. The insects began turning into miniature bombs. One by one, only a few at first, they exploded. With increasing rapidity the insects blew apart, blood and ichor spattering everywhere. Within seconds Lan had magically destroyed the physical manifestations sent to weaken him.

As the final insect burst like an overinflated balloon, Lan sensed something he had not thought possible. Claybore's fear filled the chamber like a dense, black cloud of dust.

Claybore, master mage, feared him!

Lan laughed aloud and cast forth his light mote. Like a bolt of lightning, it surged directly for Claybore's cracked, chipped skull.

"Protect me!" the mage screamed at Tefize.

Lan almost fell from the ledge when the gnome's spell smashed against his defenses. He reeled and had to brace himself against the rock wall. Lirory Tefize did not gloat

over the moment's victory; the gnome sent another coun-
terspell, which turned Lan's legs rubbery.

He toppled forward into the pit.

Lan was barely aware of swinging freely, being scooped
up in midair, and carried over to the far side of the pit.

"Friend Lan Martak, do be more careful," came Krek's
words. But Lan scarcely heard. His attentions focused solely
on the pair of sorcerers whom he battled to the death.

Death? Claybore was immortal. And Claybore had let it
slip that Lan was himself immortal. How can a battle, even
a magical one, be to the death when immortals fight?

"There is eternal pain," came the soft, vibrant words
from deep within his head. "Death is surcease. Immortality
carries infinite agony."

"Who are you?" Lan demanded. "I should recognize you
but I don't."

"Fight."

Again the voice faded from within his head, and again
he felt rejuvenated, refreshed, able to carry the battle without
swords to his enemies.

Lan sensed the strange magical twistings in the chamber
around him. Claybore prepared to use the Kinetic Sphere
to change worlds. Lan dared not let the mage go; finding
him along the Road might prove impossible without some
tangible link. To get here he had used one of Claybore's
commanders. If the sorcerer successfully shifted worlds,
locating him might take centuries—longer.

"You will regret this, Martak!" raged Claybore. The pinkly
pulsating sphere within Claybore's chest cavity glowed as
brightly as Tefize's emerald eyes; then something went
wrong. The luster changed subtly, the hue altered, the power
diminished.

Lan, Claybore, and Tefize shifted worlds but their bodies
remained firmly rooted inside the mountain kingdom of
Yerrary.

"What are you doing?" shrieked Claybore, out of control. "You will maroon us all between worlds. Do you want to be lost in the whiteness forever?"

"You had no compunction about stranding Inyx there," said Lan.

"She's only a mortal."

"What would it be like, Claybore? What would you do for all eternity trapped in a dimensionless space?" Lan fought the other sorcerer as Claybore turned new and different spells against him. They shifted worlds repeatedly—and still their bodies remained in Yerrary.

"What does he do?" asked Tefize. "This is confusing to me. We go to other worlds along the Road and yet we remain in the chamber."

"He is sapping the power of the Sphere. I don't know how. Damn you, Martak, stop that!"

Lan reached out and employed his world-shifting spells only to the Kinetic Sphere. He guessed Claybore felt as if his heart were being wrenched from his torso.

Lan took a brief moment to regroup his own powers, to muster his newfound abilities. While he didn't know for certain, he *felt* he could move between worlds now without either Kinetic Sphere or cenotaph. He was beyond physical instrumentality; he had moved to a more magical plane, transcending even that occupied by Claybore.

The headiness of this revelation left him weak with surprise and intent on putting those powers to their fullest use.

Lan Martak began a new weaving of spells but off in the distance, from a point beyond infinity, he heard, "Friend Lan Martak, what are you doing? Where are you going?"

He had no time for anything but the battle raging between worlds, throughout all time and space. A single gesture made the nagging voice vanish, a spell of dismissal to free him from the annoying spider. And Lan felt amusement rising within. He was more powerful than even the vaunted

Claybore. Mere mortals were beneath his contempt now. He could wage a magical battle and win.

Claybore would succumb to him. Soon. Very soon.

"Martak, you overreach yourself," came Tefize's words. "Look around you and note well this spot. This is your grave. You will never leave here. You cannot!"

"Don't prattle on so, gnome. Your powers do not affect me in the least."

But Lan did risk a quick glance about. He stood on a mountaintop looking out over a gently rolling plain. In the far distance rose a mountain of incalculable height, dwarfing even the rock on which he stood. That monstrous pillar rose up and gutted the sky with a dozen spikes of the purest jet protruding from its top. Of the blackness that comprised the shaft itself, Lan saw only the depths of space. This mountain of midnight was material and yet immaterial. It sucked in light and yet gave forth reflection. Heat and cold meant nothing to it and Lan Martak experienced those and more from its surface so far away.

"Look upon it and know you will never leave this world, Martak," came Tefize's softly menacing words. "It is your bane. You will die because of that. Die!"

Lan sent his light mote hurtling for the distant mountain. Incomprehensibly, the vast, thick pillar of night-black represented his destiny. But not now. Not until—what? When?

The light mote went *around-through-between* that mountain peak in some fashion Lan didn't even try to understand. The time for knowing would be soon, but not yet.

Laughter welled up, laughter all too familiar to the young warrior mage. Claybore had gained something while his attention had been diverted by the mountain.

"My powers weren't adequate before, Martak. They will be now. I didn't approve of Tefize showing you what you have just seen, but it all worked out for the best. Witness!"

Again in the rock chamber, Lan faced the gnome and

Claybore. Workers from the Tefize clan toiled to pull out a metallic case from the pit. Lan glanced over the jagged rim and down to a platform fifty feet below where more gnomes frantically dug.

How long had he stood and gazed at the column of blackness on that other world? A second? A year? However long it had been, the pause in the battle had allowed the gnomes to reach their goal.

"You will keep your promise, Claybore?" asked Lirory, oblivious to Lan's presence now.

"The arms. Give me my arms!"

"Your promise first."

"Yes, yes, of course. All that and more will be yours. Compared to these, what are a few paltry worlds?"

"You might be right," mused Lirory Tefize.

"Give them to me!"

"Very well." Lirory motioned and the gnomes pulled forth the metal-sheathed box. "You will note how well I have preserved them for you."

"Damn your eyes. Stop stalling."

Lan tried to send forth another magical attack and found himself stymied. Simply being in the presence of that metal box snuffed out his most potent attacks. When one of the gnomes opened the box and Lan saw the withered arms within, his heart leaped to his throat.

"Yes, Martak, you've lost. Oh, yes, yes, you've lost it all now." Claybore cavorted about like a madman while Lirory Tefize reached into the box and reverently lifted forth the left arm. Claybore spun and thrust the shoulder stump out. A blaze of eye-searing light filled the chamber as arm touched torso. Several of the gnomes standing too close caught fire and burned to cinders even before their screams of agony stopped echoing through Yerrary.

"And now the other," said Tefize. He reached out and stroked the mummified right arm.

"Wait," Lan said. "Claybore will never keep his promise

to you, whatever it was. Give him this power and he will be invincible. He won't need you any more. He'll kill you as he has killed millions!"

Lirory Tefize smiled, revealing broken teeth. The emerald eyes burned with manic fury.

"He will not betray me. I retain control over him. He needs more than just the arms. I have the legs, also!"

"Don't do this!" pleaded Lan.

The left arm had ignited lightning blasts that illuminated worlds. As the right touched torso, intense cold filled the chamber. Mind-numbing cold, cold from the depths of space, cold more frigid than any borne by arctic winds.

Lan watched helplessly as the arms, now firmly in their proper places, began to swell and take form. No longer desiccated, fingers wiggled and pointed. Power welled up from within Claybore, power unlike any Lan had experienced before. If Claybore had been a menace before, he was a thousandfold more so now.

Irrational fear surged and died within Lan. Claybore was immensely stronger, but he made no move to attack. Since he and Lirory Tefize had played for time to free the buried arms, there had been no new magics directed at him. Lan wondered at this, then allowed his light mote to probe forth, stinging needle-sharp at his foes.

Lirory Tefize shrieked in abject pain and rolled into a tight ball on the floor. He was not seriously injured, but he had been touched. He now knew Lan Martak still represented a formidable opponent.

Claybore's response was less pronounced, but the mage still had to struggle to retain some semblance of his aplomb.

"Y-you cannot kill me. The gnome, perhaps. Try it and you will suffer the consequences."

"Really, Claybore? Are you truly immortal? Might there not be spells to be found along the Road that will dissipate your consciousness and spread you so thin that you can never regain your present form, your present condition?"

Lan taunted the sorcerer to see the response. No magical attack came. They were stalemated, for the moment. Lirory Tefize was a sorcerer of considerable power, but now that Claybore had regained his arms, the gnome meant nothing. And Lan knew that his own power matched Claybore's— in spite of his recovering the arms. How or why he couldn't say, but Lan's power had grown, too.

Tefize's revealing the pillar of black to him had augmented his abilities, even as it had delayed him. Nothing had been gained in the exchange when he and Claybore compared relative strengths.

But compared to other mages, Lan Martak knew he was the single most capable anywhere along the Cenotaph Road. He had gone beyond warrior and mage to . . . what?

Lan Martak felt godhood within his grasp. Who else stood against Claybore? The moment of incomparable ambition passed and Lan found himself staring out into the chamber, Claybore and Tefize rapidly retreating down one of the corridors. He blasted forth a fire spell that only added wings to their feet.

Then Lan noted a new danger. The gnomes who had done such a quick job digging out Claybore's arms now circled him, approached, and menaced him with spades and pickaxes. He lifted his hand to send forth a simple spell that would freeze them in their tracks and found his arms leaden.

"Stop!" he called out, using the Voice. All the power of Claybore's magical tongue went into that command.

The gnomes still advanced.

Lan moved then as if he had been dipped in molasses. Legs moving sluggishly, he started forward, following Claybore. The gnomes lashed out, shovels smashing at his knees. He toppled onto his face.

"I'm a god!" he raged. But his powers had been depleted, just as water in a reservoir is used during a drought. Lan had no idea how long it would be until his magics came flowing back. Even the simplest of spells eluded him.

Unbelieving, he held out his hand and tried to make the elementary fire spell send sparks between his fingertips. Even before he had walked the Road he had been able to manage that much.

Not now.

An axe blade missed his head by a fraction of an inch. The gnome wielding the pickaxe cursed and struck again, this time grazing Lan. New head wounds opened and threatened to blind him.

"Krek!" he called out, but the spider was nowhere to be seen. Lan felt abandoned—then a cold chill shook his body. He remembered the faint voice coming to him during battle, begging for aid. A simple wave of the hand had dismissed such foolishness.

What had he done to Krek?

A gnome kicked him in the side, sending waves of agony washing throughout his body.

He stroked over the necklace of power stone he had been given in Wurrna. Some small measure of his magic returned, but not enough. Even this had been exhausted in his duels with Tefize and Claybore.

"Claybore has left too early, it seems," came a cold voice from further down the corridor. Lan rolled over, got to his feet, and stared at the woman, feeling nothing toward her, not even hatred. He was too exhausted for such a high level of involvement.

"It has been a while, Kiska," he said to Claybore's remaining human commander.

"It will be even longer before we meet again, Martak. You and I will meet only again in Hell!" The woman drew forth a long rapier and slashed at the air in front of her with it. The whishing noise caused the gnomes to step back. The woman's visage told them not to interfere; her hatred for Lan Martak was complete. Her victory must be, also.

"I can reduce you to a smoking cinder," said Lan, standing his ground. Kiska k'Adesina advanced, the blade's tip aimed directly between his eyes. Lan never flinched, but inside he quailed at the idea of being sliced apart. His magics had gone and his physical weakness was almost complete. He could barely stand after the magical battle.

"Do it then, worm. You killed my husband. For that I'd love to see you die the death of a thousand cuts. One small cut. Not enough to bleed to death, but painful. And another and another. Soon enough the blood would flow from you like a river, from each little scratch." She slashed at him, the sharp point cutting open his tunic and leaving a red track behind where she had lightly pinked his skin.

"Claybore wants you to kill me?" he asked, curious.

"*I* want to kill you. Claybore be damned."

"Claybore told me I'm immortal, that my magics are so great I will live forever. You can't kill me."

"Then I'll have the pleasure of hacking you to living pieces and feeding you to the dogs!"

Another cut barely missed his cheek. The steel rang loudly against the stone wall. Lan retreated. His mind worked over the energy spells he knew. This was a desperate maneuver that would leave him even weaker than he was now, but he needed a bit of magic, a spell, a small geas—anything!

"Don't do this," he said, putting all his power into using the Voice.

Kiska k'Adesina advanced, lunged. The blade slid to one side as he deftly twisted.

"I want you to resist," the brown-haired woman said. When Lan had first met her, she had chased him into the mountains. He had wondered at this mousy-appearing woman who had risen so high in Claybore's ranks, but he wondered no more. He read the insanity blazing within her like a forest fire. He might have killed her husband—he had and with grim pleasure because alLyk Surepta had murdered his lover and his sister—but this was only an excuse for the woman. If the death hadn't occurred, Kiska k'Adesina would have found some other reason, some other cause.

He again dodged her lunge.

In the chamber, near the rim, Lan looked down into the pit. It fell at least a hundred feet.

"No, worm, I won't be confused into stepping over the edge. Your magics must be dimmed or you would have used them." The smile contorting her face gave Lan a moment's rush of fear. Only great effort allowed him to settle his emotions, to think, to act.

Kiska lunged once more, point aiming true for his heart. Lan kicked out with his feet, felt the blade slide along the length of his chest, then fell heavily forward. His feet tangled the woman's. One snapped down heavily on Kiska's knee, while the other caught behind her foot. She flailed wildly before turning in air and crashing to the floor.

The battle was not to be won so easily. Like a tiger, she regained her feet, but this time without her rapier.

And a new factor entered the fight. Lan's magics were still weak, but physical power returned.

"I will *kill* you!" she shrieked, launching herself at him with fingernails drawn back into claws.

Lan grabbed a wrist, turned, and dropped to his knee. Kiska flipped over and landed hard on her back. He gave her no chance to recover her wind. He dropped onto her chest with his knee, further forcing the air from her lungs. She turned white, then flushed a bright red as she struggled for air.

As she gasped and weakly writhed on the floor, he scooped up her rapier. The first gnome coming within range died, the blade spitting him. Another ended up toppling into the pit when Lan kicked forth and landed a heavy boot on the gnome's rear.

The others turned and fled. Lan laughed, more and more physical power flooding into his body. By the time Kiska had regained her breath, Lan knew she could never again menace him.

Physically he was as fit as he had ever been—and his magics seeped back.

The only blot on his victory was Claybore's recovery of both arms. But Lan pushed that from his mind. He had held off both Claybore and his captive mage Lirory Tefize. He could defeat them again.

And he would.

CHAPTER SEVEN

"That's not possible," Inyx said forcefully. Her words stung the spider more than she intended. Even larger tears beaded at the corners of the huge dun-colored eyes before spilling over to drip onto the floor. Inyx went to Krek and put her arms around his chitinous thorax. He shook her off.

"Friend Inyx, this is the end for me. I have endured so much in my life, but always have I thought Lan Martak's allegiance to me a permanent one. I was wrong! I have been wrong about so many things. Why did I ever stray from my web? Why, oh why?"

Ducasien shuffled nervously nearby, his hand rubbing over sword hilt. He appeared unsure whether to draw and hack at the giant arachnid, run, or stay and listen.

Inyx left Krek momentarily and whispered to the man from her own home world.

"He is distraught. Lan has done something to him. A spell, perhaps. I don't know why he'd do such a thing, but we have to find out. The two of them have been fast friends for longer than I have known Lan."

"He is rather large, isn't he?" Ducasien said, eyeing the

spider. Krek shivered and collapsed into an even smaller bundle on the floor. His long legs sprawled gracelessly, making him look like a felled tree with its roots pulled from the ground.

"You've never been on a world with the mountain spiders?" Inyx raised one eyebrow in surprise, then remembered how few worlds she'd seen with the spiders. Without Krek and Lan accompanying her, she might never have found even a single valley filled with the monstrous webs and the incredibly fragile-appearing aerial walkways traveled by the beasts.

"I've seen some odd things, but nothing to compare."

"He's not odd," she snapped. "Sorry," Inyx said in a softer tone. "This is making me edgy. I can understand swordplay. I can even understand courtly intrigues and the backstabbing of politics, but dealing with Krek is different." She turned toward Ducasien and almost whispered, "He's my friend."

"You don't want to see him hurt. I understand that," said Ducasien. "How can I help?"

"What? You don't have to. This isn't your fight."

"I want to make it my fight," he said, looking directly into her vivid blue eyes. Inyx felt the current of emotion flowing between them and fought it. She didn't want it. Not like this. She had other battles to fight, other loves to win— loves that had been won. Lan wandered inside this hollowed mountain, needing her. That he had dismissed Krek in such a cavalier fashion indicated that.

Not for a moment did Inyx believe Lan had abandoned Krek. Put a geas on him to save him, yes. That was fully within her powers to understand. Lan might even have said something in the heat of battle that the spider had misinterpreted. Krek's mind was not human; his thoughts followed devious paths not shared by nonarachnids.

"Krek," she said, "tell me everything that happened."

The spider lamented a bit further, then finally unraveled the tale of battle at the rim of the pit.

"... the ledge crumbled away so I swung out on a strand of web and dangled over the pit waiting for him. When I called, he ... he dismissed me."

"Do you remember his exact words?" asked Ducasien.

Krek turned one eye toward the man and said, "I do not know you."

Inyx spoke quickly to introduce them. Krek remained in his despondent state.

"I ask only to help you," said Ducasien. "There might be a clue in the manner of his speech, the way he said the words. After all, you were in mortal combat. The slightest of mistakes might have meant both your deaths."

"That is the odd thing," said Krek. "Claybore said that Lan Martak could never die. It ... it affected him so strangely. He both grew in stature and shrank."

"Shrank?" asked Inyx, puzzled.

"He took on greater magical abilities. I felt the ebb and flow of his power as if it were some palpable force. But something fled from within him, too. He became diminished from what he had been."

"That's the answer," said Inyx. "Claybore cast a spell on him."

"I sense magic. The tide of battle did not go in that direction. This was something within Lan Martak. And that was when he tossed me aside like a well-gnawed insect carcass." Krek pulled in his long legs until he occupied a space hardly larger than the length of Inyx's sword. Anyone passing by in the corridor might even mistake Krek for a coppery colored boulder.

"What do you think?" Inyx asked of Ducasien.

"Magic is alien to me. I know only what I have overheard and most of that is boast or outright lie. Never have I actually confronted a sorcerer."

"You are new along the Road," said Inyx. "In spite of what Krek says, I don't think Lan willingly chased him off. To protect him, yes. To warn us, yes. But I know Lan. He would never ignore a friend in need."

"People change," said Ducasien.

Inyx turned and her eyes flashed angrily.

"Lan did it to protect him. I know it."

Ducasien fell silent and Inyx's anger cooled. She worked over the events in her mind and came to an uneasy realization. Lan Martak *had* changed since she'd met him. While their love had deepened and taken on an intimacy she had never dreamed of—the mental link between them when they were together revealed both their most intimate thoughts— Lan was not the man she had met so long ago. He had grown and in that growth had changed. His magical powers demanded more of him than she'd thought any human could deliver. He had delivered and kept on growing in ability.

Had he reached the point where he no longer controlled the forces flowing about him? Did the magics now control him?

"Could he truly be immortal?" asked Ducasien, breaking the woman's train of thought. "I have heard of such but, well, I believed those to be wild tales told over a mug of wine."

"Immortal? Lan? Hardly," she said, but the words rang hollow and she felt fear gripping at her belly. The cold within refused to go away because Inyx worried that Lan might have become more than mortal. Immortal? If so, he was lost to her forever. She would be only an ephemera in his life, a moment's diversion in an eternity of experience. Would he even remember her name in a thousand years? In a hundred?

She shook off such nonsense. Lan was not immortal.

"There are—" began Ducasien, but his words were cut off by a wild cry echoing down the stony corridor. The sound of heavy boots clattered and scraped against rock and soon enough Broit Heresler stumbled into view.

"Help," he gasped out. "We have been attacked. The Tefize clan invaded our territory. They try to kill us all!"

The gnome had been battered almost beyond recognition. Crimson flowed in spurting streams over his face and soaked his collar and shoulders. His right hand rested limply within his tunic and his left arm carried a deep cut caked over with dried blood.

"You know this one?" asked Ducasien, his sword out and pointed at Broit.

"Yes, he befriended us outside. We fought together and then got separated within the mountain."

"Which clan is he?" asked Ducasien.

"Heresler. The gravediggers." Inyx saw the tall man relax a bit, his sword point dropping from target. "What do you know of them?"

"They are friendly enough," Ducasien answered, "and have helped me a time or two. The Tefize kill any who stray into their corridors. The Nichi are little better."

"You'll come to our assistance?" asked Broit Heresler, falling to his knees and almost fainting from the pain caused by his wounds.

"Inyx?" The man looked at the dark-haired woman for her response.

"We'll help. What else can we do? We need friends inside Yerrary and the Hereslers are our best bet."

"The Heresler clan will not forget this. We will give you the finest funeral, the best grave site, the most pallbearers of any of those whom we have buried. I promise it!"

"How touching," Ducasien said dryly.

"It's their life," said Inyx, cautioning the man not to make further comment on this. "Where is the fighting?"

Broit Heresler pointed in the direction he had come.

"Krek? Will you aid us? Our friends need us."

"Lan Martak does not need us. He does not need me. He told me to go away as if I were a mere spider, a servant; worse!"

"I need you. The Heresler clan needs you. And we'll find Lan and get this straightened out."

"There is nothing to straighten out, friend Inyx." Krek heaved himself to his feet and shook like a dog just out of a pond. "Of course I will fight alongside you. You are all that I have left."

Inyx didn't want to argue with the spider. She patted him on one nearby leg and then helped Broit Heresler to his feet. The gnome tottered precariously but showed more strength in walking than she'd given him credit for. The rolling gait reminded her of a sailor long at sea finally come ashore, but Broit managed to make good time in spite of his unsteadiness caused by his wounds. Within minutes she heard the first sounds of battle.

A surge of anticipation seized the woman. She had been raised for combat. Her hand tightened on the hilt of her sword, then she took a deep breath. Inyx let out a blood-curdling yowl of attack, then rushed forward.

Her frontal attack momentarily scattered the Tefize and gave Broit a chance to regroup his beleaguered grave-diggers. Inyx swung her sword in a smooth, economical arc, cutting at wrists and necks, lunging for exposed throats and groins, and even occasionally lancing through to an eyeball. In minutes her blade dripped gore.

Ducasien came to stand beside her, guarding her left, giving her encouragement.

"You fight like a legion. There is no way they can defeat us if you keep up this pace!"

Inyx flashed him a smile, then said, "Shut up and fight, dammit. They'll swarm over us like locusts if we don't account for more of them soon." Inyx disengaged her blade from a probing broom handle, cut over, and lunged. The Tefize gnome let out a gusty sigh as he died—but another rushed forward to take his place. And another and another.

Even with Ducasien helping, Inyx found herself being beaten back. The crush of numbers overwhelmed them and their position.

Inyx shouted out to Broit Heresler, "We need to retreat. Lead the way to a safer spot where we can make a stand."

"There is no safer spot," the gravedigger moaned out, clutching his injured right arm. *"This* is the heart of Heresler territory."

Inyx took the opportunity to glance about her. If this was the Heresler stronghold, they were indeed in serious trouble. Everywhere she looked lay dead gnomes—all diggers— and the phosphorescent moss growing on ceilings and walls had been ripped off in many spots, giving an eerie cast to all that happened within the chamber.

Death moved in green-glowing shadows.

The Tefize launched a redoubled attack that bowled Inyx over. She lost her sword and pulled forth her dagger to hamstring and jab at muscular bodies washing over her— but the woman knew it was all in vain. They had her and would quickly destroy her.

"Aieeee!" came the shrill cry. Inyx's head almost split from the reverberation in the closed chamber, but her heart beat so hard it almost exploded in her chest.

"Krek!" she called. "Here!"

The mountain arachnid lumbered forward, mandibles clacking like a scythe against grain. Gnome after gnome perished. Krek cared little whether they were Tefize or Heresler; if they stood in his way, they died, but for the most part they were Tefize.

"I've never seen a fighting machine like that," muttered Ducasien, stopping to stare as Krek slashed his bloody way into the center of the room. Even though the spider stood hunched over, he managed to reach out with his legs and rake talons over exposed bodies. Gnomes by the score died before they could flee.

Within the span of another frenzied heartbeat, the Tefize clan fell into disordered retreat, shrieking and pointing, dropping their crude weapons, and disappearing into minor corridors too small for Krek to follow.

Looking aloof, the spider simply stood in the center of the chamber as if nothing had happened and shook off the sanguinary gore.

"You are the mightiest warrior I have ever seen," complimented Ducasien. "May I shake your hand?"

Krek canted his head to one side and studied the man with a saucer-sized eye.

"You are another of those silly humans unable to perceive I have no hands. But if you want to take my right front leg, you may do so. I feel it is a strange custom, but one with which I am not unacquainted, after enduring it on other worlds."

Krek lifted the indicated leg and held it out for Ducasien. The man took hold and shook solemnly.

"It is my privilege to name you my friend," the man said.

"You defended friend Inyx quite well, from all appearances," Krek said, looking over Ducasien's shoulder at the pile of dead. "If for nothing else, that elevates you to the exalted position of my friend." The spider bobbed up and down, then said, "Friend Ducasien, is she well? She still lies on the floor in a most unflattering pose."

"Inyx!" the man cried.

"I'm all right," Inyx said, struggling to sit up. Bodies piled across her held her until she managed to wiggle free. "I'm a little bruised, nothing more."

"Are you sure?"

For an instant their eyes locked. Inyx uncomfortably broke off the gaze. It spoke too much of things she did not wish to pursue.

"Of course I'm sure. Help me to my feet." Inyx staggered

slightly, then saw the cut along her upper thigh. "I need some help binding that, but otherwise I'm still in fighting trim."

"I'll tend the wound," said Ducasien, but before the man took a single step forward Krek pushed between the pair.

"One moment. A bandage is required. I am most expert at such matters."

"I'll . . ." started Ducasien, then fell silent. In fascination he watched as Krek reached out with surprisingly gentle strokes and cut away the cloth around Inyx's wound. Inyx cleansed her own wound and then Krek spat forth sticky webstuff that pulled the jagged edges of the gaping cut together. The flesh held in place, the spider spun forth a cocoon of the finest silk. Inyx's leg was neatly bandaged in less than a minute.

"The silk will decay soon and fall off within a week. By then you should be well healed."

"That's amazing," said Ducasien. "How do you do it?"

"I'm a spider," Krek said indignantly. "The silk is meant to fall apart within a week so my hatchlings can get at the cocooned food, not that I consider friend Inyx in such a light, mind you. This is merely an application that occurred to me some time ago when I noted how often you humans damaged yourselves."

"Lan doesn't need such bandagings," spoke up Inyx. "He can heal himself—and us, too—magically." Even as she said the words, the woman knew she'd made a grave error reminding Krek of how little Lan needed him, even for menial tasks like this. She reached out and laid a gentle hand on the spider's nearest leg and said, "Krek, I need you. And I'm sure Lan does, also."

The spider turned away. Every footstep left a bloodied mark to show his passage down a side corridor.

"Where's he going?" piped up Broit Heresler. "We want to have a celebration. For all of you. You've saved our homeland. And look at the work you give us," the gnome declared, looking at the bodies stacked about the chamber. "No shirking our jobs now!"

"The victory won't last for long," said Ducasien, "unless we can build some barricades to hold them back. With your depleted numbers another attack might be the last."

"We're getting even with them," the gnome said defiantly. "We're not going to bury any of *their* bodies. See how that sits with Lirory Tefize! This'll be ample warning to the other clans, too, that we Heresler don't fool around. We mean business."

"What Ducasien means is that you're the ones going to be buried if the Tefize attack again. There're only a few of you left."

"Us buried? Don't be ridiculous. If all the Heresler are dead, there won't be any more gravediggers." As if this thought hadn't occurred to the gnome before, he turned pale at the idea. "Great Yerrary, that'd mean chaos. Disaster. Dead bodies everywhere."

"Someone else would take over the job," said Ducasien.

"They can't. Each chore is specialized, hereditary. Only Heresler bury. This might be the demise of Yerrary if they kill us all off. Oh, no!"

Broit gathered the pitiful few survivors around him and they spoke hurriedly, gesticulating wildly. Fear began to show on their wrinkled faces as the full impact of what defeat meant penetrated.

Ducasien and Inyx walked around the chamber and saw sleeping pallets placed in shallow depressions in the rock walls, a few possessions, odds and ends indicating living quarters rather than simply another corridor. They exchanged sad glances and walked on. This was no fit way to live, hidden under tons of rock and never seeing the sky. On their home world it had been different. The seasons were kind, game was plentiful, and all were able to live as they chose, free and in the soft lemon sunlight.

The gnomes in Yerrary existed in conditions totally alien to Inyx and Ducasien.

"We could block off this passage," Ducasien said. "That leaves only those four ways in. A waist-high barricade would slow down a full-force attack."

"Better to string fang-wire and let the bastards cut themselves to ribbons if they attack."

"I didn't see much evidence of metalworking," said Ducasien. "Fang-wire requires at least low-grade steel to do any good."

"They must have wire around. When I found the source of their drinking water, the entire chamber was filled with glass and metal vats, tubes and pipes. I don't remember seeing wire, but Eckalt must use it somewhere."

"Eckalt?"

Inyx explained to Ducasien about the toad-being and his distillation plant. Ducasien shook his head in puzzlement.

"This is a strange world, unlike any I have seen along the Road. I think I have seen enough of it."

"You'd move on?" Inyx asked, sudden fear clutching at her throat.

"You want me to stay? For a while?"

Again Inyx averted her eyes from his. She didn't trust herself to speak. She only nodded.

"Then I'll stay. For a while. And to make that stay safer, we'd best get to work. Do you think the gnomes would take kindly to a few suggestions about defending their pitiful little fortress?"

"Let's see."

Inyx went and spoke at length with Broit Heresler and several of the surviving clan leaders. In time she convinced them to erect barricades as Ducasien had suggested. While they had no fang-wire or anything similar to it, Broit did show Inyx how razor-edged digging implements could be placed in traps along the corridors. The unwary might set off these devices and end up minus a hand or head.

"Confusing," admitted Ducasien. "No wire to speak of, but they use the best of steel for cutting edges. Drawing wire wouldn't be hard and weaving it with the barbed points would be simplicity in itself."

"I doubt that," said Inyx. "These folk have existed for centuries like this. Their culture is stable and any intrusion is looked upon as a catastrophe. That's why this civil war is so upsetting to them. Lirory Tefize has been bitten by the worst bug of all—he seeks power."

"As I said before, I've had little contact with mages. It strikes me as peculiar a mage of such power would be found among them."

Inyx watched as Broit and the others bustled about dragging stones and digging pits. These were a people of physical attributes, not magical ones.

"I agree, but magic stretches between the worlds. Perhaps Lirory Tefize tasted it on some other world."

"They don't strike me as travelers, either."

"One walks the Road for many reasons."

"There is glory," the man said.

"Adventure is more like it. Who can know of your triumphs if you only pass through on your way to another world?"

"Knowledge," said Ducasien. "It's a portable wealth far transcending gold and jewels."

"Knowledge is two-edged and cuts the unwary. A better reason is curiosity. What lies beyond the next cenotaph? A better world? A world of jest or sorrow? One covered with oceans or deserts or mountains and paradise?"

"You've seen them all, haven't you?" Ducasien asked.

They sat on a small ledge cut into the wall and leaned back, the green glowing moss soft against their tired backs.

"I've seen more than my share. Ever since I met Krek and Lan, the worlds have become more deadly. Claybore's influence stretches over most of them."

"But you fight well against the sorcerer," insisted Ducasien. "You are the mightiest warrior I have ever seen. Your blade work is superb and your sense of tactic unparalleled."

"You're just saying that," Inyx said, feeling a blush rising.

"I say it because it is the truth. You are a remarkable woman. That you are from my own world is all the more delightful "

Inyx swallowed hard when Ducasien reached out and placed his finger under her chin and turned her face to his. She felt as if her heart would burst from her chest. Hands shaking, she tried to push away. Ducasien held her firmly and moved closer. Their lips brushed in a kiss both gentle and electric. Inyx melted within and then remembered.

Lan Martak. Somewhere in the bowels of this mountain her lover battled Claybore. He might be close to death; he might desperately need her fighting prowess of which Ducasien boasted.

Inyx pulled away and stood, face flushed.

"I'd best find Krek and make certain he is all right. The spider tends to mope." She didn't wait for the man's reply. She almost ran away. But she couldn't flee her innermost emotions.

CHAPTER EIGHT

"Are you so taken by your new appendages that you let *him* remain alive?" Lirory Tefize looked back over his shoulder in the direction of the chamber he and Claybore left. "This Lan Martak withstood our combined assaults, but I felt his power seeping away. Another attack and he will perish. I know it."

"Do not be so certain. Martak draws on more than his own power. *I* felt *that*. No, Lirory, we must be more subtle." Claybore swung about on his mechanical hips and waved his arms joyously. "They are wondrous," he said. "After so many years I cannot describe the way I feel regaining my arms."

Tefize watched as the fleshless skull turned full attention to the air in front of them. Claybore's hands gestured and the air itself began to boil and churn. The dual death beams leaping from his sunken eye sockets joined the turbulence. Even as inured as Lirory Tefize was to displays of magic, he cringed away from the beast Claybore conjured.

Simply looking at it turned the gnome inside out. His stomach churned unpleasantly and thoughts both dark and vile rose within him. If a mere glance produced such an unsettling effect, what could the creature do if released?

Tefize tried not to think of that.

"Is she not a beauty?" Claybore cackled. Hands moving with dextrous skill, the sorcerer molded the very air. The ruby beams mingled intimately and gave substance to the creation until it stood on stubby legs tipped with vicious-looking talons.

"What is it?"

"There is no name for this fine little pet. It exists and yet it does not. Parts of it live on other worlds along the Road, while the majority of it rests here. The conjuration is one of the most difficult I know. It must be supported on all those worlds to be effective in this one."

Tefize glanced back at the chamber where Lan Martak stood. The gnome hated leaving unfinished business like this. Even worse, the human would soon enough regain his considerable power and seek them out in the maze of tunnels worming through the mountain. Tefize did not relish the idea of sleeping with guard spells fully in place to warn him of an enemy's approach.

"Send your beast against Martak," he suggested to Claybore. "Let us see how deadly this ghostly creature can be."

"Nonsense," said Claybore. "Martak is of no current concern to us. Let him wander about trying to do his odd jobs. We can finish him off when the time is ripe."

"You gloat. That is senseless." The gnome tried to control his rising anger. "Do not think to play with him. I felt his power. He held both of us at bay—*both* of us. If I had not risked showing him the Pillar of Night, my excavators would never have retrieved your arms in time."

"Yes, showing Martak the Pillar did gain us time. I rather liked the idea, too. Let him see his destiny. Let him see the weapon of his destruction!"

"You peer into the future?" asked Tefize. His skeptical tones caused Claybore to whirl about. Mechanical legs grated and gears snapped, but the organic upper portion of his body moved with sinuous grace. The only unnerving part was the fleshless skull still perched atop the torso. While Claybore had never mentioned it, Lirory had discovered that Martak and the others were responsible for the destruction of Claybore's face and other skin.

"I cannot see the future. That is perpetually closed to me, but I know the present. You worry overmuch about Martak." Claybore's fingers wove a set of glowing interlocked triangles in the air. The shadow creature he had conjured snarled and started for Lirory.

The gnome stepped back, felt cold rock against his spine, and began defensive movements. He had walked myriad worlds, seeking knowledge. Alone of all those populating Yerrary he had accumulated vast magical lore, but even his most potent spells failed to stop the inexorable advance of Claybore's beast.

Lirory Tefize stared at it in wonder and horror. His vision went *through* its pseudo-flesh and stared out onto a thousand other worlds, yet the substantial fangs and talons ripping gouges in the rock floor were all too real. Eyes of black blazed with strange emotion.

What did such a beast feel? Tefize only guessed it had to be frustration, anger, hatred at all living beings existing on only one world.

The eyes opened onto all those worlds and, at the same, remained curiously flat.

Tefize straightened, trying to avoid the claws as one misty paw raked outward toward him. The lightest of touches on his belly sent chills racing to his very soul.

"It cannot be killed because it does not live. Not exactly. Let Martak conjure his elementals. They exist only on one plane. My friend crosses over into many!"

Tefize heard the insanity in Claybore's tone, but did not respond to it. The deceptively small magical creature hunkered down in front of him, gathering strength for a leap at his throat. Tefize muttered continual protective wards now. It seemed that each was sucked into a bottomless vortex and only the creature remained. Unharmed. Raging at all material life.

"Do not harm him, my little one," soothed Claybore. "Lirory is our friend. Aren't you, Lirory?"

"Friendship is a word too strong to describe our relationship, Claybore," said the sorcerer gnome. "Let us say our relationship is based on mutual distrust and personal greed."

"Greed? No, not you, Lirory. Not I. We are beyond greed for material things. We seek power, that heady wine of which there is no fill." Claybore cackled and motioned, leaving red and green streamers behind from each fingertip. The shadow hound backed away, eyes still boring into Tefize.

"We deal for mutual gain," said Lirory, his uneasiness fading now. He still had what Claybore desired most in all the universe. Without the legs, the sorcerer would never come close to realizing his ambition. The magically powered mechanical contraption holding torso, arms, and skull would break down all too soon. Even the most casual of observers could see the bent struts and rusted gearwheels.

And beyond mere movement, his real legs contributed to Claybore's magics.

"It will require some time to retrieve your legs," said Lirory Tefize. "After I found the arms, I took great care to place them in the pit where no casual seeker would stumble over them. With your legs, I exercised even more diligence in hiding them."

"Really?" said Claybore. The sorcerer spun around on mechanical knees, the ruby beams seeking forth from empty eye sockets. The death rays launched themselves through rock in an upward direction. "My legs are along this path."

"Of course you can sense their presence," Tefize said suavely, hiding his consternation at Claybore's easy discovery. "Getting them free without damaging them is something else again. I assure you the spells are intricate."

"The legs cannot be destroyed," said Claybore.

"You lie," snapped Lirory. "But even if that were true, they can be hidden along the Road. My spell will throw them at random onto another world. You can seek them out, yes. But have you the hundreds—or thousands—of years to do so?"

"I am immortal."

"You claimed Martak was, also. Will he give you the chance to go hunting?" Lirory Tefize shrewdly discerned the reaction in the dismembered sorcerer and saw he had struck a nerve. "Martak's power grows daily without need of retrieving his bodily parts. If you desire more magics, you must recover other segments of your original self."

"You will get your worlds to rule," snapped Claybore. "I have promised this."

"What game are you playing with Martak? Why didn't you destroy him when you had the chance? Playing a cat and mouse with one so dangerous is foolhardy."

"If he bothers you so, Lirory, go and eliminate him. You have my permission."

Lirory Tefize studied the cracked, chipped skull for some hint of treachery. No glimmering of emotion showed to give a clue as to Claybore's motives, but the gnome felt secure as long as he controlled the mage's legs. Giving up the arms had been necessary to defeat Martak—temporarily—but Claybore would pay dearly for his legs. Dearly, indeed.

"You will not care if I destroy him?" asked Tefize.

"I've already dispatched one of my lieutenants to do so. If you can aid her, fine. Do so." Claybore made a small motion of dismissal. Tefize almost staggered under the magical impact of that gesture. That brought home to him how dangerous was the game he played; but the gnome had defeated all the other mages of Yerrary. Claybore would prove no different.

"This lieutenant of yours," he asked. "I assume it is the woman, Kiska k'Adesina?"

"Her hatred for Martak knows no limits. I decided to give him to her as a token of my gratitude for her loyalty."

Lirory knew the other sorcerer lied. Whatever went on, it would be more complicated than simply allowing one of his commanders sporting a hate for Martak to vent it. But what? Lirory Tefize didn't know.

"Martak will die," he said, regaining his balance and starting back for the chamber. Already the gnome formed the spells that would reduce the upstart mage to a smoldering cinder. The human was adequate in his spells, but Lirory had experience. And with exhaustion preventing Martak from fully conjuring at the height of his ability, Tefize had no doubt the battle would end quickly, as it should have before.

Claybore watched his ally depart. If that fleshless skull had possessed lips, they would have been drawn back in a sardonic smirk. Claybore turned in the direction of his legs, bathed in their wondrous radiance, pivoted, and went in a different direction, heading downward inside the hollowed-out mountain, down, down, down to the bowels of Yerrary.

Claybore followed a path through the tumbled rock and partially excavated passages, his metallic legs clicking with effort. But his newly rewon arms aided him. A pass here, a gesture there and rocks turned to dust. He used precious energy in this display of magic, but the mage didn't care. Simply having the power once more was an end in and of itself.

The gnomes had neglected this portion of their mountain keep for decades—perhaps longer. Dust lay heavily wherever Claybore stepped, but the skull did not breathe, did not sneeze as the clouds billowed up around his hideous half-human, half-mechanized form. As he approached a small rock cairn, his steps slowed. Finally halting a few paces away, he simply stared at the ancient heap.

Ruby beams lashed out at the rock pile and blasted it to gravel. Beneath where the rocks had been lay a cavity rimmed with a low wall, a pit dropping into the center of the planet itself. Claybore hesitantly advanced. Gone was all bravado. The shows of power were past. As much as any time in his existence he felt fear now, real fear at what lay trapped within this pit.

The sorcerer bent forward at the hips and peered into the infinite blackness of the pit. He saw nothing. Spinning suddenly, his death beams lashing forth, he sighted on a small rodent. The creature let out a frenzied squeal, then keeled over. Claybore gently picked up the stunned form and squeezed with his hands. The feel of fur and living flesh beneath his fingers after so many eons thrilled him. He wanted to keep squeezing until life crushed from the rat. But he stopped. There was a better use for the creature.

He cast the feebly kicking form into the pit.

From far off something stirred. Darkness took shape and flowed, billowed, became a thing living as it sucked the vitality from the tiny blood offering.

"You seek?" came a deeply resonant voice.

"You know I do," snapped Claybore. His fear knew no bounds at what lay within, but his anger at the pettiness overrode it.

"You have not changed in the millennia I have known you, Claybore," said the Resident of the Pit.

"I've seen your shrines on a thousand worlds, Resident. I have spat on every one of them."

"Really, Claybore? Since Terrill sundered your parts, that must have required great magics on your part." A rumbling chuckle boomed from the depths.

"Terrill is no more. And you are trapped within. How does it feel to be a god and to lack power? Not to have worshippers believe in you? You scorn me but I live, I move freely. You are trapped, Resident of the Pit."

"Scorn? Yes, I feel that and more," admitted the Resident. "But trapped? Hardly. I *am* a god and I am everywhere. On this world and on every other one in the universe."

"Are you on this world?" cried Claybore. His hands wove quickly in front of him. Above the pit appeared the same vision Lan Martak had seen. The ebony spire rose high above the plains on a world; sharp spikes radiated from the top of the pillar.

"The Pillar of Night," sighed the Resident of the Pit. "You know I am there, more than any other place."

"You know who put you there!"

"Your triumph will be short-lived, Claybore."

"Short-lived?" Again Claybore laughed aloud, as much to release fear as in true mirth. "You have been trapped for ten thousand years. You call that short?"

Almost imperceptibly came the answer, "Yes."

Claybore did not hear. He drew himself up to full height and bellowed forth his triumph at what he had done to his enemy. The Resident of the Pit had aided Terrill in his dismembering magics, but it had cost Terrill more than his life and had allowed Claybore the chance to imprison a god. A god!

"You think to repeat your trick, using Lan Martak as your catspaw this time," said Claybore. "It won't work. He is a weak vessel for your magics and lacks the ability Terrill had. You cannot pour in power without rupturing him. Martak will fail, Resident, and you will remain imprisoned for another ten thousand years."

"Lan Martak has stood against you thus far," said the Resident of the Pit.

"He cannot be victorious when I have regained my legs. Even with only my arms in place, I feel the power on me. I feel it!" Claybore glowed all over in the reddish hue emanating from the eye sockets in his skull.

"A petty trick hardly worthy of even an apprentice mage. Such tricks do not impress me," said the Resident.

"Yes," sneered Claybore. "I keep forgetting. You are a *god*."

Again, a whisper, "Yes."

"My reign will span a million worlds—more! Power undreamed of will be mine. My legions already conquer most worlds along the Road. In time, they will all bow to me."

"What then, Claybore? Have you thought of the consequences of winning? After you rule all worlds, what possible new goal can there be? What of the boredom then, not being able to achieve anything else in all the universe?"

Claybore fell silent at this. Never had he considered the question. His fight for dominance had been too long, too bitter, too demanding to think of the future. For an immortal, being bored posed major problems.

"It will take many millennia before that happens. By then, I may have a new adversary."

"You would create one to crush?" asked the imprisoned god.

"Perhaps. If it pleased me. Until then, I will cherish the power I wield. All will bend their knee to me. Never since the creation of the universe will so many cry allegiance to one being."

"You would be a god, also?"

"I am one, fool. I am not trapped in a pathetic hole in the ground. I am immortal. No matter what forces you bring to bear—what powers you give Martak—I cannot be slain. Terrill discovered that to his regret. He no longer exists as a human; I lived and will live forever!"

"Your words take on shrillness, Claybore. Do you truly believe that?"

"It is the truth. Admit it is the truth!"

"Is this a question you ask of me?"

Claybore laughed at the Resident of the Pit.

"I forgot. You've been reduced to little more than a wishing well, haven't you? You must answer whatever questions are posed to you. Imprisonment has its penalties, doesn't it, Resident?"

"Yes."

"Very well. Is it not the truth that I will live forever?"

Stirrings in the blackness in the pit showed the turmoil felt by the god trapped within.

"You will live forever," came the slow words.

Claybore laughed and laughed and laughed.

"Tell me one further thing. Will I triumph over Lan Martak and go on to rule all the worlds along the Cenotaph Road?"

"Lan Martak will know infinite sorrow because of your doings, Claybore," came the baleful words. "I feel my vitality slipping away. The life-offering you made was insufficient to maintain me on this world for long."

"Go on, then. Slip off to your real prison. And know who has done this to you. It is I, Claybore!"

The shadows twisting in the pit stilled and only clammy, dead air remained in the chamber. Claybore laughed harshly one last time, spun on his mechanical legs, and stalked away. The Resident of the Pit had told him he would be victorious. His spells imprisoning a god—a god!—forced the Resident to always tell the truth when asked a question.

Claybore thrilled in the knowledge of invincibility. Even his bitterest enemy had admitted it!

"With a single twist I can break your neck," Lan Martak told the captive woman. Kiska k'Adesina struggled in his grip, but failed to find a weakness. The man's magic may have been drained for the moment, but his physical strength surpassed her own. She stopped fighting and hung limp in his stranglehold.

"What are you going to do with me?" she demanded.

"I ought to go ahead and snap your neck." Lan thought furiously about what he would do with the woman. She was an enemy sworn to killing him in the most foul way possible.

Turning her loose was ridiculous, yet he couldn't bring himself to slay her in cold blood.

But wasn't that exactly what Kiska would do to him, given the chance?

He shoved her onto hands and knees and picked up her rapier. Holding it lightly between thumb and forefinger, he moved the point around in tight circles. One single lunge would end a life—of a foe.

Something moved within him that prevented the lunge and thrust. To kill her in this fashion would mean he was no better than she. He fought for freedom from Claybore's tyranny; to kill Kiska k'Adesina in this fashion was to give in to the very principles he hated most.

"Go on, coward," she taunted. "End my life. Unless your manhood has withered and died."

"There's a better way," Lan said.

"What?"

"I don't know," he admitted, "but killing you isn't it."

"Your black-haired slut would not hesitate."

Lan had to agree. Inyx's sword would have leaped from its sheath in a smooth silver arc and made a deadly connection with Kiska's throat. In such matters Inyx was much more like the spider Krek.

"Release her," came the cold words from off to his right. Lan spun, sword at ready. Lirory Tefize stood in the corridor, hands hidden inside his tunic. The gnome's face pulled into a grimace of distaste that caused Lan to pause for just a moment.

"Where's Claybore?" he asked.

"Release k'Adesina," repeated Tefize. "Do so and I will spare your miserable life."

Lan knew better than to believe a mage, much less Claybore's captive one. Wasn't this gnome the one responsible for giving back Claybore's arms?

Lan spun and got behind Kiska, the blade resting lightly across her throat.

"She dies unless you leave."

"An idle threat," Tefize said angrily. "You had the chance to kill her and didn't, for whatever reason. I believe it is because you are weak. And what makes you think she matters at all to me? She is Claybore's pawn, not mine. She matters even less to me."

"Kill us both, Tefize," cried Kiska. "Just be sure he is dead."

"Shut up," Lan said, pulling the sword edge back harder across the woman's throat. To the sorcerer he said, "You are more talk than before. Can it be you're afraid to cast a spell for fear of injuring her? What would Claybore do to you if you harmed her? She's important to him. She's his sole remaining commander."

"She means nothing to Claybore," Tefize said flatly.

Lan had to admit the gnome was right. He began backing away, taking Kiska with him. Her thin body provided scant protection from a magical attack and barely more from a physical one.

"Do not think to evade me so easily," said Lirory Tefize. He lifted his hands and began a low incantation. Lan felt the magics rising about him like the ocean in a tidal basin. And with the magic came a twisting feeling within unlike anything he had ever experienced. It grew from the magic and yet was apart from it. He didn't understand what it was that affected him so.

But with the churning in his gut came a trickle of his own magical power. He hurled forth a protective spell that snuffed out Tefize's assault totally. And using this as cover, Lan pulled the woman with him down a side corridor. His powers were still too feeble for a real attack and he had no desire to only fend off whatever spells Tefize cast in his direction.

"Die, worm," muttered Kiska k'Adesina. "Let the short one kill you. He will be more merciful than I when I get the chance."

Lan frowned at her words. They were familiar enough, but the tone changed subtly. Gone was the stark hatred and replacing it was—what? He didn't know. The sharp edge of her insane need for revenge had been blunted somehow.

"This way," he said, dragging her down another corridor and another and another. Behind he felt magical heat. Lirory Tefize's spells dogged their footsteps and still he lacked the strength to properly fend off the other mage. Lan knew better than to risk a physical attack. Such turned against the sword-wielder with the suddenness of a summer storm. Better to play for time until he regained his own powers.

The weight of Lirory's magics built up on him, though, until he barely managed to stagger. Deadly bolts of lightning ravaged the walls of Yerrary. Heat turned rock to slag. Pits opened almost beneath his feet, causing Lan to choose other paths through the mountain. And all the while he felt the changings within himself. Every time he formulated a spell of his own, the tickling sensation grew and confounded him even more.

It did not sap his strength. It grew as his magical strength grew, but did not hinder him in any way. Lan cast it from his mind. Never before had he been so drained after a battle. This must be a compensation he had not been sensitive enough to feel before.

"He's getting closer," said Kiska.

"Afraid?"

She turned brown eyes to him that caused the feeling within his breast to stir even more.

"I won't let Tefize hurt you," he said, his voice almost choking him.

"Martak!" came the mage's taunting challenge. "Stand and fight! I will reduce you to a smoking cinder."

Heat blossomed in every doorway, trapping Lan and Kiska in the center of a chamber. Molten rock dripped down and blocked any possible escape, even if they had been able to enter one of the tunnels.

"What are we going to do?" asked Kiska. "He's trapped us."

Lan smiled. His light mote bobbed in the far distance, a distance of the mind rather than of space. He teased it along until his familiar came ever closer.

"There's a way out. Up there." He pointed to the rock ceiling.

"But it's solid," protested Kiska. "How can we..."

The light mote surged upward and drilled effortlessly through stone and burst out of Yerrary. Cold air gushed down and bathed their sweat-soaked bodies. A second gust of wind robbed Tefize's heat spell of even more power.

"Up. We go up."

"But that's outside the mountain," said Kiska. "We can't live out there. It's too dangerous!"

Lan didn't point out to her that staying within Yerrary was even more dangerous. He had recovered from his gargantuan battles with Tefize and Claybore, but not enough, not soon enough. There had to be a rest period to nurse himself back to full strength and ability.

Arm circling Kiska's trim waist, Lan rushed straight upward on a solid plug of rock rising from the floor. His mote spun in a network of light as it drilled free the rock plug and lifted. They burst onto the slopes of the mountain and staggered forward onto loose stone, stumbling and falling down into a ravine.

"Tefize will follow," said Lan. "We must be ready for him."

"No, he won't follow," said Kiska. "The gnomes hide within their mountain and seldom venture out. For them those tunnels are the entire world."

"Tefize is a sorcerer."

"It matters naught. He will not follow."

Lan sent his mote scouting and discovered the woman was correct. Lirory Tefize stood under the hole carved in the roof of his protective mountain and simply stared up at the nighttime sky. Lan recalled his light mote when Tefize stalked off through the corridors of Yerrary on his way to rejoin Claybore.

"We're safe," Lan said, leaning back against cold rock. "It's hard to believe he wouldn't carry the fight outside."

"Is it?" asked Kiska. "This is an inhospitable world. Look at the storms."

In the far distance electrical discharges raged that made even his and Claybore's pale in comparison. He sighed. The battles had been desperate and he was tired to the core of his being. Only a single acid droplet spattering on his forehead prevented him from slipping off to sleep. The burning brought Lan fully awake and aware.

He glanced over at Kiska k'Adesina huddling in the lee of a rock, protecting herself from the beginning rains. She was his enemy—but he felt protective toward her. Lan shook his head. There was no accounting for what tiredness did to him.

He lifted the light mote and spread it like an umbrella over both of them. Kiska moved closer, as if he might use the rapier on her at any instant.

"There, there," he said. "Everything is going to be all right. Just relax. We'll find a way back into the mountain and—watch out!"

Lan Martak spun about, sword flashing through the mist. He slashed frantically at the fire-breathing lizard that slithered down the ravine at them—he slashed and missed.

"Damn the fog," he muttered. "The creature uses it to hide."

"What creature?" asked Kiska, her hands stroking his arm.

"That one!"

Lan pushed the woman behind him and went to do battle with the huge lizard beast menacing them. Finding it in the fog became more and more difficult and he soon forgot about Kiska or reentering Yerrary or anything else at all.

CHAPTER NINE

Lirory Tefize gazed up into the blackly billowing storm clouds crowning his mountain kingdom. The acids poured forth and flooded through the hole carved by Martak; off to one side the gnome saw the thick gatherings of fog sweeping down the ravine where Lan Martak had taken refuge.

"Good enough," the mage said to himself. "They will trouble me no more. What Claybore failed to do, I have done. Driving Martak outside is sufficient to destroy him in his present condition."

Tefize again checked and saw that magic usage from outside was minimal—not enough to save Martak from the insidious mind-altering effects of the fog. The gnome closed his eyes and built the proper spell. Heat blossomed forth and washed over him. Rock melted and flowed, closing the opening. In minutes no trace of the hole remained. The phosphorescent moss visibly crept back to cover the spot, seeking a source of heat for growth.

The gnome's attention turned to other matters. Dealing with Claybore proved more and more difficult. The sorcerer's newfound power on regaining his arms worried

Tefize, but not overly. He had taken a chance giving those limbs back, but it had been a calculated risk. Lan Martak's power had been extraordinary. Only with Claybore augmented by new bodily parts had they managed to triumph.

But would Claybore give him the power he promised? Tefize doubted it possible for the mage to say anything without lying. It came as second nature to him. But using the mage's legs as a bargaining point had certain advantages. What would Claybore do to regain them? Was control of a dozen worlds too large a price to pay for control of thousands, or even millions?

Lirory Tefize didn't think so. With proper choosing of those worlds to rule, he decided it would be less than ten years before his own power rivaled Claybore's. Traveling the Road had shown the gnome much. Careful lists compiled to show each nexus of power would come in handy very, very soon. Control those points, gain strength and knowledge, depose Claybore.

The disembodied sorcerer might be immortal, but Lirory Tefize knew that Claybore had been defeated once. A second time was possible—and this time the victor would not perish as Terrill had.

Tefize smiled and turned; then stopped. A frown wrinkled his forehead and anger welled inside him.

"Master," came a weak voice. "We have been defeated."

Lirory Tefize faced one of his clan. The gnome abasing himself was bloodied and barely able to crawl forward.

"What happened?" Lirory demanded. "How could the Heresler have beaten you? You followed my plan to the letter, did you not?"

"Master, they had help. Two of them with swords. And the spider! Never have we fought so well and died so nobly; but the spider!" The gnome shook all over and buried his face in his gnarled hands.

"Oh, get up. Stop groveling," Lirory said irritably. Dealing with such incompetence was a burden he disliked heartily. Ever since he had killed or exiled the other sorcerers from Yerrary, greater and greater demands of leadership fell upon him. It seemed that no one accomplished anything now without his personal guidance. Would it be like this when Claybore relinquished control of those worlds to him? Lirory Tefize didn't want to consider that at the moment.

"Where are they? The spider and the others who so ignominiously trounced you?"

"Master, they are in the Heresler territory."

Lirory stalked off, stubby arms crossed over his barrel chest. As he walked he thought and frowned even more. He found no residual effects of magic. However his clansmen had been defeated, it wasn't through the use of the arcane. In a way, this bothered him more than it should. He expected treachery from Claybore—he didn't put it past the mage to aid one side over the other to sow discord. To defeat a force undoubtedly without equal in all of Yerrary through purely physical means wrought havoc on the troops and their morale.

Lirory felt control slipping away. He did not like the feeling.

Stopping short of a junction leading into Heresler-controlled corridors, he closed his eyes and listened. In the distance he heard faint scratching noises, rock against rock.

"They put up barricades," he said to his clansman. The battered gnome only bobbed his head, whether from fear or in agreement Lirory couldn't tell. The mage began tracing patterns in the air before him, lines that first glowed pale blue and finally took on an intensity that caused his clansman to shield his eyes. Lirory Tefize stared directly into the center of the burning rectangle he'd formed.

Swirls of color took on substance, changed, flowed again, and finally came into focus. Lirory muttered a final spell and then watched the small picture and the gnomes busily working within the fiery frame.

"Master, that is Broit!" cried the gnome.

"Silence." Lirory spoke in an offhand manner. He focused all his attention on the picture and had scant time for dealing with subordinates. The barricades being erected by the Heresler clan were adequate to thwart a simple frontal assault. Lirory knew such an attack was out of the question. Using this clansman as a guideline, the mage knew the Tefize would never be whipped into attacking. They were defeated both physically and in morale.

But there were other routes open to him.

"Those large ones. The humans. They were responsible for your defeat?" he asked.

"The spider, also."

"Yes, there is the spider." Lirory repressed a shiver of disgust. The monster crouched to one side of his magical viewing port and slowly masticated a cave roach. Lirory turned his port away from the arachnid and back to Inyx and Ducasien.

"What are you to do, Master? Do . . . do we attack again?" The obvious fear in the gnome's voice solidified Lirory's belief that the Tefize clan would be defeated in any further fight.

"*I* attack. You and the others need only enter after I am victorious. The Heresler will not trouble you."

"You send demons to them?" The eagerness stemmed more from seeing an enemy vanquished than in releasing such potent magical beings. Lirory wanted to shake the gnome until the broken teeth rattled for even mentioning such a course of action. Elementals, demons, magical beings from other planes were all dangerous conjurations.

He did shudder convulsively as he remembered the shadow hound Claybore had summoned forth with his newly regained arms.

"There are other spells. The large sorcerer is not with them," Lirory said smugly. "I have already taken care of him."

"Master!"

"Do not fear. He has been cast outside Yerrary. The fog has seized his mind. He will never threaten us again."

"Master, you will reign supreme forever! Your power knows no bounds!"

"Of course it doesn't," Lorory said in distraction. He knew the tales of defeating Lan Martak would spread and grow with each reverently whispered retelling. Good. Before the end of this year the name of Lirory Tefize would linger on everyone's lips, some speaking in fear, some in awe, and all in total obeisance.

Lirory worked up the power required for the binding spell he would use. To project through the magical window was the only way possible for him. His magics were limited in that he needed to see the object of his spell. Lirory wondered if it were true that Claybore could project spells without seeing his victim. If so, that made the disembodied mage even more dangerous than he appeared—which was deadly, indeed.

Inyx and Ducasien sat close by one another. Good. That made it easier for him to cast a single spell to capture both. While Lirory was certain it lay within his power to form two equally effective spells and direct them to different targets, this made his work all the easier.

"They . . . they shimmer, Master!" said the watching gnome. Awe tinted his voice, but Lirory was beyond feeling pleased at this. He needed every particle of his being to propel his conjurings now.

"Tangles," he muttered. "Feet numbing. Fingers tingling. Stand, yes, that's it, stand and try to shake off the effects." Lirory smiled broadly now. Both Inyx and Ducasien played into his hand by fighting the paralyzing spell. If they had stayed quiet he might have failed. Not now, not with them beginning to experience the first feathery touches of his spell.

Inyx opened her mouth and emitted a scream that echoed down the hallway. From the burning framed picture there came no sound. She spun about wildly, slapping her hands against her body. Every turn caused her increasing dizziness until she collapsed in a heap on the floor.

Ducasien tried to kneel beside her, to aid her. He bent forward and kept going. He crashed heavily atop her, unable to do more than feebly twitch.

"The Hereslers will not oppose you now," said Lirory. "Get a small party together. We go in to retrieve our two guests."

The gnome hastened away and returned a few minutes later with a scruffy band more fearful than anxious to serve. Lirory silently motioned them forward. It was a measure of his control that they obeyed. To have refused meant even worse punishment than death at the hands of the large ones allying themselves with the Heresler.

Lirory Tefize moved the viewing port around and found the spider. Spell after spell wove through the air and bound the arachnid's feet together. When Krek sensed the first of the Tefize clan at the barriers, he attempted to stand. The spells held him firmly.

"But he is so different," muttered Lirory. He tried other spells to render Krek totally unconscious and all failed. Finally he gave up on the attempt. Keeping the spider pinned to the ground, his deadly long talon-tipped legs powerless, was almost as good as being able to kill him magically.

Lirory turned to the Heresler gnomes hacking and cutting at his own clansmen. Pass after pass sent the defending gnomes reeling backwards. Lirory felt drained to the center of his being by the time the Tefize had conquered the Heresler.

On shaking legs, he walked forward, then paused and stiffened his resolve. It did not do to show weakness before an enemy—or an ally. With haughty contempt, he strutted into the center of the Heresler clan territory and slowly turned, looking at the captives.

"Well done, my friends," he complimented.

Even though they had done little, the Tefize clan's morale rose. They puffed out their chests and bullied their captives.

"This day will long be remembered in our clan tales," Lirory went on. Even though his knees threatened to lock and send him toppling face forward onto the ground, he walked about congratulating the gnomes individually and glaring at Broit Heresler along the way. When he came to Krek, Lirory stopped and stared.

Krek's legs were still tangled with the numbing spells he had used, but his mandibles clacked ferociously. Lirory made a point of standing well back. One quick snap of those death scythes might sever head from torso. He started a new spell, one workable at close range, and then stopped. Dizziness passed through him and threatened to make the gnome mage fall into a faint.

"Leave the spider," he said, fighting his weariness. Lirory knew it would take hours to regenerate power. How had that large one Lan Martak held off the combined magical attacks of Claybore and himself? It hardly seemed possible in the face of his own exhaustion now. But Martak was long dead. The creatures thriving on the exterior slopes of Yerrary were not gentle. And after breathing the mind-twisting fog and feeling the acid rains burn skin and set fire to the very rock, there was no way Martak could live.

"What of *them,* Master?"

Lirory looked at Inyx and Ducasien, then allowed himself to slowly smile.

"Bring them. And as for the others of the Heresler clan, they are permitted to live."

Broit Heresler spat at the mage and missed.

Lirory went on as if nothing had happened, saying, "They will be permitted to live as vassals of the Tefize. See to it that they are given appropriate jobs."

"There won't be any of us who'll dig your grave, Lirory," cried Broit Heresler. "See how long it takes the cave worms to gnaw your bones. None of us will go outside and give your corpse a proper burial. Wait and see!"

Lirory gestured that the Hereslers be taken away. The giddiness still bothered him. He needed to return to his throne of power and replenish his energy—soon.

"Don't bother with lifting them. Drag them. It's easier." He took a perverse glee out of seeing Inyx and Ducasien dragged along the rough rock corridors. This more than anything else kept the mage moving with a sprightly step, his bandy legs pumping along quickly to keep up with his clansmen.

Several turnings later, they entered an area strictly Tefize. Down two levels, past the trough of rainwater pouring in from outside, and to the new excavations they went. Finally Lirory stopped and pointed to a rock cell.

"There. Place them inside."

Inyx and Ducasien were semi-lucid now, moaning and weakly thrashing about. In minutes they would fight off the effects of his numbing spell. Lirory watched, summoned his modicum of remaining power, then bound them magically to the rock cell. Try as they might now, they would never be able to leave this small, stony enclosure.

"What did you do to us?" asked Ducasien. The man sat up and held his head. Lirory knew it had to be splitting wide open. That was one delightful aftermath of his nerve-numbing spell.

"That is of little concern to you. You should be more worried about what you are to do next. There is no escape from this cell for you. None. You will die within it. No food, no water. Or rather," Lirory said, chuckling evilly, "the water isn't very good for drinking."

He pointed. High above Ducasien and Inyx the cell roof peaked up and showed a small patch of the cloud-riddled nighttime sky. Rain blew into the opening and dribbled down the walls.

"If a real storm blows up, this cell might fill with water."

"It can't. It'd go out the doorway," Ducasien said. To

human vision there was nothing barring the way. To Lirory's magical sight, however, a barrier firmly blocked anything material from passing.

"Think, large one. We shout at one another, as if we talk through walls. Is that not so?"

Ducasien shoved himself forward, got his feet under him, and lurched toward Lirory. The gnome simply stood, waiting, watching, smirking. Ducasien let out a scream of infinite agony as his hands touched the magical sheet stretched tightly over the opening.

"It will prevent water from leaving the cell," repeated Lirory. "Rains come, fill up, the acids burn away your flesh. Yes, that is what might happen—if you are lucky."

"And if we're unlucky," Inyx said, managing to croak out the words.

"Ah, dear lady, if you do not pray for a storm to end your miserable lives you will linger for a long, long time. No food, you know."

"We might die of thirst first."

"So be it," said Lirory, enjoying this.

"What's to keep us from climbing out?" asked Ducasien.

"Nothing." Lirory smiled wickedly. If they tried that, the water seeping down the rock would surely burn their fingers severely and, if luck rode with them and they reached the top somehow, the opening wasn't large enough for either to crawl through. The finest mountain climbers had tried to escape this cell and had failed. Neither Ducasien nor Inyx would live for longer than a week—or even through the storm growing outside.

"Lan will save us. He can just wave his hand and make this barrier vanish."

"Yes, dear, dead lady, he might be able to do so. If he lived. He does not."

"You lie! You short, bowlegged, wart-ridden bastard! You're lying!"

Lirory said nothing more. Let the dark-haired woman

rage. It only added to her torture. He now had to return to his throne of power. Without rejuvenation he would keel over all too soon. With as deliberate a move as possible, Lirory Tefize whipped his cloak over one shoulder, spun, and walked off, never looking back at his two prisoners.

The mage felt nothing but satisfaction at this day's work. With his clan enemies removed, he had only Claybore to contend with. And soon, very soon, Lirory Tefize's name would be bannered—feared!—across a score of worlds.

"How long?" asked Ducasien, pacing to and fro in the cell.

"There's no way to tell." Inyx nervously looked above to the tiny opening in the rocky ceiling. Wind whirled drop-lets of the acid into the air and the morning sun caused bright rainbows to form, rainbows of death.

"There's a way out of this. There has to be."

"Rest. Save your strength. Lan will come for us."

"Your faith in him is so great?" Ducasien stared at her in open wonder.

Inyx didn't reply. She wondered if Lirory had been right about killing Lan. It hardly seemed likely. Lan Martak had withstood mages hundreds of times more powerful—he had endured the worst Claybore had to give and still lived.

But perhaps the gnome spoke the truth. Perhaps they were doomed.

Inyx tried to shake the feelings of dread mounting within. Lan ought to have found them by now. It had been hours and hours. To give up hope meant Lirory Tefize triumphed all the more.

"We might never leave here alive," said Ducasien in a low voice.

"That worries you?"

"I have regrets," the man said, sitting beside Inyx on the floor.

"What regrets? Things you've done?"

"Things I haven't done."

Their eyes locked again. This time Inyx didn't turn away. She couldn't. She held the same fears that Ducasien did. Whether it was because he understood her, being of her own world, or whether the nearness of death drew them together she didn't know. The attraction was apparent—and mutual.

Ducasien leaned forward and lightly brushed his lips across hers.

"I . . . I need more," she said in a weak voice.

"Then I will die without any regrets at all," he said.

Arms locked about one another, they embraced and kissed deeply. Their weight shifted and they lay side by side on the hard rock floor. Neither noticed. Fingers explored, probed, stroked, caressed, excited. Clothing slowly opened, exposing new territories for their mutual pleasure. And soon enough their bodies merged into one writhing, undulating mass of desire.

"No more regrets," whispered Ducasien.

"None," answered Inyx. Then words were no longer possible.

Krek tried to stand and fell heavily, only rising to half his full height. The numbness had left his front legs sooner than his rear ones. Twisting his thorax in a painful maneuver, he forced his inner juices to flow into his limbs.

"There," the spider said, heaving himself aloft. While still wobbly, he was able to walk about the chamber that had formerly housed the Heresler clan. All the gnomes had been packed off to servitude under the Tefize now. Why he had been spared, he didn't know; that he had, only confirmed that humans and near humans were peculiar folk.

"A real spider would have eaten me while I was paralyzed," he said. "So much for their ruthlessness. Now where have Inyx and her new foundling gotten off to?"

Krek regained strength as he walked and by the time he homed in on the magical curtain holding Inyx and Ducasien prisoner, he felt the usual spring returning to his stride. Only the low corridor ceilings prevented him from bouncing along as he'd have liked.

"Friend Inyx," Krek called loudly when he saw her sitting disconsolately within the cell. She did not answer or even give the slightest notice of him. He lumbered to the magical barrier and examined it as well as he could. Krek was no mage, but he sensed magics of a permanent nature.

While this shimmering sheet lacked the potency of a cenotaph, it had a permanence to it that told the spider that waiting for the magics to dissipate was a mistake.

"Inyx!" he called as loudly as he could. She did not move.

Ducasien walked back and forth, hands clasped behind him. The man looked aloft nervously from time to time. Krek bent down and peered upward. The sight of acid rain dripping down the rock caused the arachnid to shudder.

"My friends, you are in a sorry state. Allow me to aid you, if I can." He began digging beside the magical screen in hope of penetrating the rock. Whether Lirory had imbued it with magical toughness or whether the rock was naturally strong, Krek didn't know. All that mattered was his inability to dig through it.

"Might I swing down through that opening?" he wondered aloud, again looking upward at the tiny vent in the cell's roof. Krek blinked at that idea. To drop a web down into the cell required him to venture outside. In the rain. With the mind-confusing fog.

"But I cannot allow you to languish in that awful cell. It is nothing but cold rock and that hideous burning water leaks from the very walls. Not even a fit spot to string a web within."

Krek tried futilely to again attract Inyx's or Ducasien's attention and then gave up on the effort. Only one course of action suggested itself. He had to locate Lan Martak and bring him down here to rescue Ducasien and Inyx—soon.

Humans were such frail creatures he didn't know if the two within the cell would survive much longer.

Krek blinked and began turning about, looking for other magical beacons. Faint hints came from above. Krek went up through Yerrary, one level at a time, seeking out Lan Martak. When he finally reached a vaulted chamber with openings along the walls, he stopped. To pass through any of those doors meant he would find himself outside the warm bulk of protecting rock.

"Friend Lan Martak," he said, almost sobbing as he mouthed the name. He remembered how Lan had abandoned him, left him to fend for himself in the middle of battle. How he had used a spell to dismiss him like some lowly servant. To seek out the mage took more courage than Krek thought he possessed. His pride had been damaged—and even worse, his friendship betrayed.

"Friend Inyx needs my help," the spider said. "And without Lan Martak there can be no aid." He blinked again and saw flickers of magic outside. Lan Martak was nearby, out in the rain and fog, his magics intermittently flashing like the lightning arcing through the nighttime sky.

"Water," sobbed Krek. Then the spider plunged through one of the openings and out onto the slopes of Yerrary.

The rains pelted the mountaintop, setting the very rock afire. Krek saw thin streamers of fire rising from every spot where a droplet of rain struck ground—a double horror for him. Water and fire. He rubbed his furred legs together anxiously and then saw real trouble ahead.

Thick banks of fog drifted languidly down the mountainside. And within one of the fog clouds came distinct indication of Lan Martak and his magics.

"The fog affects humans as well as spiders," he told himself. But Krek fought down the need to return to the relative safety of Yerrary. Inyx needed his aid and retrieving Lan Martak was the only way that help could be given. No matter that Lan Martak had betrayed his trust. No matter anything. Krek fought to remain true to his friendship with Inyx.

She needed him. He plunged forth, talons clacking against the hard, acid-pitted stone of the mountain.

"Lan Martak!" the spider called out. The only answer he received was muffled cries from within the fog.

Krek stopped and looked down into a ravine filled with the mind-altering fog. He saw creatures lurking just behind the cloaking veils of mist, creatures so horrific his mind refused to believe in their existence. Krek tried holding his breath in the hope that this would make the beasts go away.

They only moved closer, as the fog rose up along the ravine walls.

"Lan Martak!" he called again. "Can you hear me? Friend Inyx needs your magic." He refrained from adding how much he needed to renew the bonds of their friendship, to find the cause for Lan's dereliction during battle.

"Krek?" came the faint question. "So many enemies. They're everywhere. Huge lizards. Fighting them. So tired. Can't keep going much longer."

"Keep talking," Krek ordered. His sense of hearing was acute, but his sensing of vibration even more acute. Talons dug into the corroded, acid-pitted rock. He turned slowly until he found the source of the words, the bootsteps against rock, the clanging of steel into stone.

"Too many of them. Too tired to use more magic. They're everywhere. Aieee!" The shriek rose to taunt Krek. The spider used all the sensory information he had and then launched a hunting web into the fog. It missed. He tried again and again.

Finally he caught something.

Krek hesitated to reel in his catch. While he truly thought the mist creatures were products of the fog and not reality, he wasn't certain. He might be pulling one of those ponderous beasts directly to him.

Krek jerked hard and a thin—and human—body sailed forth to crash into the rock at his feet.

"Kiska k'Adesina!" he cried in surprise.

The woman stared up, dazed and unable to speak. Krek spat forth an amber drop of solvent and freed her from his hunting web. For a second he worried that she might have slain Lan Martak. A new cry of anguish from the man's throat came to the spider—and a new web rocketed forth to vanish into the grey, swirling depths of the fog.

This time Krek pulled out a weakly struggling Lan Martak.

"Hurry," Krek commanded. "The rains are coming." A single look at the ferocious sky confirmed this. Both Kiska and Lan stumbled and moved like they were possessed by demons. Movement, no matter how clumsy and uncoordinated, toward the entrances to Yerrary soon carried them to safety.

Lan sat wild-eyed and simply stared at Krek.

"Is the fog still upon you?" asked the spider. He dared not name this man friend again. Not yet.

"The visions," Lan said slowly. "They're fading. They . . . they were so real!"

"Have you recovered sufficiently?" pressed Krek.

"What's wrong?"

"Friend Inyx is imprisoned below. Only you have the power to free her."

Lan Martak didn't reply. He sat and clutched himself, hands convulsively squeezing his upper arms. Looking around, his eyes finally focusing, he stared downward through the rock floor.

"Claybore," he muttered.

"Lan," started Kiska k'Adesina. A slash from Krek's mandibles forced her against the wall. She paled and licked her lips nervously. But she didn't speak further.

"Claybore is down there," Lan said. "And I sense more.

His legs. Yes, the emanations have to be from his legs. He will regain them if I don't hurry."

"Lan Martak, Inyx is in desperate need. Free her, then go after Claybore."

Lan Martak turned and stared into the spider's dun-colored eyes and said, "I can't help her. Not until I've defeated Claybore."

"Without you, she'll die," pressed the spider.

"Then she must die. I must find Claybore and finish him before he finds his legs. I must." Lan rose and staggered off. Kiska k'Adesina came and supported him.

Krek only stared in disbelief. In his arachnid brain he understood betrayal by one whom he had thought his friend. But now Lan Martak refused even Inyx. Without him she would die and still the mage refused her aid.

Tears welled in Krek's eyes for lost friends.

CHAPTER TEN

"You must rescue her. She is in need!" Krek protested. But the set expression on Lan Martak's face told the story. The mage was not rushing to Inyx's aid. He had set himself a task that required finishing before all else—anything else in the entire universe.

"Claybore is growing more powerful," Lan said, not hearing the spider. "My powers are still weak, but they return swiftly enough. The stay in the fog did little to help me, but soon I will be strong again. And it must be done right the first time or Claybore will again slip away."

"Rest, Lan," soothed Kiska k'Adesina. "The fog has turned our brains against us. I still see visions of things that are not true. You must see them also. Rest. Take your time in this."

"I must attack. Now!"

The spider stared in stark disbelief at the man who had been his friend. This Lan Martak was different, too different to bear. He was driven, haunted; the spider didn't have words to express the emotions he saw playing out their scenes on Lan's face.

Krek had witnessed spiders going insane and did not pretend to understand the cause. One day they would swing wild and free on their gigantic webs, relishing the feel of wind through their furry legs, seeing the ground so far below their mountainous kingdom and then the next the spiders would spin off-pattern, asymmetrical webs confusing to the eye and impossible to walk. Soon after the spiders might even leave their precious webs entirely and drop to the ground, easy prey for creatures prowling below.

Krek himself had touched insanity and paid dearly for it. Instead of remaining behind with his dear bride Klawn and allowing her to devour him to provide sustenance and protection for his hatchlings, he had left. He had walked the Cenotaph Road and met humans with different ways of looking at life, different mores, different values. And just when Krek thought he was beginning to understand and truly admire them—Lan Martak in particular—the man had changed drastically.

Krek tried to liken it to a spider spinning an ungeometric web and then simply abandoning all that had been held dear. The comparison failed.

By what the spider knew about humans, the bond formed between Lan and Inyx had been unbreakable.

Krek almost cried in frustration and suppressed rage when he realized he had been totally wrong. Whatever there was between Inyx and Lan, it was not love. A lover would never do such a thing as Lan Martak did now. To abandon Inyx was totally out of character—and Krek was forced to admit he did not understand the slightest portion of human behavior.

"Lan, you're overtired. Rest. Claybore will not regain his parts soon," whispered Kiska, who occasionally glared at Krek.

"You listen to this one, Lan Martak?" asked Krek. "She is your sworn enemy. *Our* sworn enemy."

Lan opened his mouth to speak, then snapped it shut

again. Confusion crossed his face and he shook his head.

"She's harmless," he said. "As long as I watch over her, she won't get into any mischief."

"She gives you bad counsel," said Krek.

"I know," the mage said, voice almost breaking.

"Then we rescue Inyx!"

"We attack *Claybore!*" contradicted Lan.

The spider fell silent. Things were not to his liking and even became more confusing as time went on. To tolerate Kiska k'Adesina's continued life bewildered the spider. One quick slash with his mandibles would remove one of Claybore's top commanders and an avowed enemy. Many had been the time when Kiska had followed and had tried to destroy them. Why did Lan Martak allow her to live now?

Lan made magical passes in the air and then spoke. Krek shivered as the mage used the Voice, the tongue taken from Claybore's own mouth. The resonance billowed up and filled the huge stone chamber until Krek wanted to shrilly cry out for mercy. This was a potent spell being cast.

And it drew Kiska k'Adesina closer and closer to Lan in some fashion Krek couldn't understand.

Soon, the young sorcerer stood with his arm protectively around her waist. Her head rested against his shoulder and her thin hand stroked up and down his arm as he watched the conjuration take form in the center of the chamber.

"There he is," said Lan. "This spell produces Claybore's image without allowing him to know he is being spied upon."

"Inyx needs you," Krek said doggedly. "We must rescue her—*you* must, for I cannot get past the ward spells the gnome mage established."

"Claybore is unprepared. Look around him. He is plotting something and it is not battle. Now is the time. I know it!"

"Lan Martak, do not do this. She befuddles your mind. Her words confuse you just as the fog did."

"Kiska's not urging me to attack. Listen to her, Krek. She's telling me just the opposite. She wants me to forget about Claybore—and I can't. We attack now."

"We?" asked the spider, standing fully upright and peering down at Lan and Kiska.

Lan swung about and stared up at Krek.

"Aren't you with me?"

"Why will you not rescue Inyx?"

"You've got a single-minded determination of how to succeed, Krek, that is faulty. Attack Claybore; then all else falls into place. We can win. We can. I know it."

"I will stand beside you," Krek said. The spider's mind turned over all that had happened and he finally decided he owed Lan Martak this one last loyalty. If Lan Martak had been a spider, Krek's decision would have been far easier— he would have eaten him. But being a human complicated matters. Humans tended to do things in definitely barbaric ways. Perhaps this was another such case, though how Krek couldn't say.

He may have been single-minded as Lan Martak accused, but Krek knew that Inyx and her friend Ducasien would perish all too soon unless something was done about the magical barrier imprisoning them.

"Krek," said Lan in a low voice as Kiska went on a few paces ahead of them, "I want to apologize."

"It is friend Inyx who requires the apology," said Krek.

"No, not this. I'm right about this. Before. When Claybore and Lirory Tefize and I were trying to reduce one another to rubble."

"The pit where Claybore's arms were?"

"Yes, then," said Lan. "I think I may have cast a spell on you when I didn't mean to. I used the Voice to tell you to leave me alone. I . . . I didn't even realize I was doing it. See, I was occupied with them and you kept bothering me and making you go away was the easiest thing for me. So, I just *told* you to leave me alone."

Krek sniffed loudly but said nothing. He had felt the spell forcing him away from Lan. But Lan Martak had cast it of his own free will. He had wanted to be alone in his fight with the other mages. The spider could do little about that, even if he did want to aid his friend—his former friend.

"I was distracted," Lan went on, his eyes moving from Krek to the slender form of Kiska k'Adesina ahead. "Claybore kept me occupied with new and diabolically different spells. I had to prevent him from regaining his arms."

"You failed," the spider pointed out. "You told me to go away and let you be and you failed."

"I said I was sorry, dammit," Lan snapped irritably. "I've got powers that sometimes slip away from me. I'm not used to using them. Not yet. You were bothering me so I told you to go away—but with too much force."

"Too much magical force," corrected Krek.

"Too much magic," said Lan, his fists clenched tightly now. The arachnid saw the growing tension in the man and fell silent. He had so much he wanted to say to Lan Martak, but not now, not within hearing of their mortal enemy. Kiska continued striding along as if she didn't have a care in the world.

Krek considered eating her, then put the thought from his mind. Lan Martak would be angry over that—and the spider didn't know the reason. On other worlds Lan had often mentioned how ruthlessly Kiska k'Adesina pursued and how equal ruthlessness would have to be used to triumph over her. Why allow her to accompany them, especially now when they went to fight her master? Krek started to ask this when Lan held up a restraining hand.

The spider stopped and stood.

"Ahead. I sense him," said Lan.

The arachnid also felt the tinglings of magic—from the Kinetic Sphere buried within Claybore's breast. The world-shifting device touched on the magics Krek was most sensitive to.

"Claybore is off some distance in that direction," said Krek, lifting a long front leg and pointing away to the right.

"Not Claybore. I want to eliminate Lirory Tefize first. The pair of them together was almost more than I could handle. Get rid of Lirory, then Claybore. I don't think Claybore can stand alone against me, even with his arms."

"You take on more than you should," observed the spider. "Forget this nonsense for the moment. Free friend Inyx and then the three of us can properly enter battle."

"Where's the spiderish bloodthirstiness I'm always hearing about? You wanting out of this?" asked Lan.

"Battle does not thrill me, not the way you humans wage it. You refuse to eat the vanquished. Why bother, except that they would kill you first?"

"Lirory Tefize regains his power too rapidly. He has some magical device to aid him," said Lan, lost in the upcoming battle. He walked as if in a trance and stopped beside Kiska k'Adesina. The woman took his arm and held it, more like a lover than an avowed enemy.

The arachnid only watched in concern. He had never fully understood human mating rituals. To his mind, they had been observed and consummated between Lan Martak and Inyx. But now Lan Martak acted as if Kiska were of great importance to him as a friend and lover. Krek wobbled about and finally gave up trying to get to the root of Lan Martak's motivations.

"He's resting in his chamber," said Lan in a low voice. "I must attack now."

"You'll attract Claybore's attention," warned Kiska k'Adesina.

"Stay here with Krek. You'll be all right."

"Why do you care about her at all, Lan Martak?" asked the spider. "She wishes you only harm."

Lan didn't answer. He faced a blank wall and began muttering his chants of power. The rock began flowing, first in tiny rivulets, then in wrist-thick rivers. The hole grew larger and larger until finally even Krek could walk through it into Lirory Tefize's chambers.

The gnome let out a shriek of pure anguish and almost dived across the room, twisting in midair to seat himself on a large slag rock throne. Only when he had both hands on the armrests did the gnome allow himself to smile.

"You still live, Martak. Your resourcefulness astounds me. Few of us even here in Yerrary can survive the fog."

Krek said, "He had considerable help." Lirory ignored the spider, his attention fully on Lan.

"Since you did not graciously die outside my mountain, you must stain its floors by dying within."

Lan laughed harshly, the sound totally unlike anything Krek had heard from the sorcerer's lips before. Mixed together with the Voice powered by the metal tongue resting within his mouth came contempt, derision, even hatred not borne of Lan's own soul.

Lirory scowled, then began a chant pitched too low for Krek to hear. The air within the high-roofed, pyramid-shaped chamber took on an electric tension as the magics sizzled.

Lan stepped forward, but Lirory held him at bay. The very rock throne on which the gnome sat began to glow bright green. The gnome mage's entire body tensed as he absorbed the aura and focused it toward Lan, who turned it aside with magical shields of his own. Only when he was sure his own strength was sufficient did Lan initiate his attack. And a prodigious one it was.

Krek flinched away as the air writhed with half-born elementals, creatures ripped from other worlds, shadowy beings lunging and slashing at Lirory Tefize. The gnome's face clouded with fear at the sight; Lan had instinctively known what produced the most panic in his opponent. They traded spells, but the outcome quickly became obvious to the spider: deadlock.

As swiftly as the spider realized it, so did Lirory. The gnome shifted weight slightly in his throne and directed a paralyzing blast straight for Krek. The lumbering creature had no time at all to avoid the spell, even if he could have. Speed meant little against the magics used within this chamber.

"Lan Martak," Krek moaned out. "My legs are again frozen. He reduces me to a pathetic heap of fur!"

Lan glanced over his shoulder, then looked back at Lirory. Kiska came and stood by the man's side, as if the pair of them fought Lirory. Krek thought the battle lost now. Kiska would distract Lan and Lirory would magically annihilate him—this was, after all, what Kiska k'Adesina had strived for across so many worlds.

"Away, Krek," came the Voice. "Get away from here!"

The spider's entire body rippled with pain as Lan gave the command he had delivered before. The overwhelming urge to leave seized Krek, shook him, forced him to move first one leg and then the other. Nothing counted except getting away from Lan Martak.

Lirory began sweating. The emerald glow of his throne took on a deeper hue as power surged through the gnome.

"You can't best me," said Lan. The mage's face remained unwrinkled with exertion or doubt. No perspiration ran down his forehead. Lirory's very fingers dug fiercely into the stone armrests as he fought against Lan's implacable defenses, his potent offenses.

"I am better," the gnome grated out between clenched teeth. "I *am!*"

Krek's pain mounted as he fought to obey Lan's command in spite of the nerve-numbing spell Lirory cast over him. Krek finally got away, his huge bulk tumbling through the hole in the wall and out into the corridor. Once outside Lirory's huge stone chamber, all traces of the gnome's spell vanished.

Inside, however, the magical battle continued to rage in ways Krek would never understand. But what he did understand was that a deadlock was again forming—unless he could somehow divert Lirory's attention. Lan needed more time to regain his strength; Lirory drew too heavily from the power base in his throne to allow Lan to completely triumph.

Krek spat out a climbing web. The bright silver dot tipping the web arched up and found a protruding stone from the pyramidal apex forming the ceiling. The dot of adhesive hit the stone, spattered across, and firmly held the web strand. Krek squeezed forward, keeping his body as compact as possible, then launched himself. He swung a short distance before scuttling aloft on his thin strand of webstuff. In seconds he dangled over Lirory's throne, directly under the apex.

The spider's immense bulk caused the gnome to nervously glance overhead from time to time. This decreased the mage's ability to continually counter Lan's magical thrusts effectively. But when Krek came hurtling downward on the end of his web, Lirory Tefize's nerve broke and he shot from the throne as if propelled by springs.

The instant that contact was lost between his body and the power-giving throne, the gnome knew he had made a fatal error.

"Martak, please, no!" the gnome shrieked.

But it was too late for him.

A fire elemental *whooshed* into existence around the gnome's stocky body, whirled twice, and then shrieked in triumph as it leaped upward, trailing flames as it went. Lirory Tefize turned to ash under the intense heat of the salamander. Krek screamed as the flaming mass rocketed upward toward him.

Lan waved his hand almost contemptuously and the elemental vanished inches from the spider and the inflammable webbing.

Krek dropped to the floor and said, "You nearly allowed it to devour me, as it did Lirory."

"I stopped it in time. What are you worrying about?"

Krek crouched down, pulling legs in tightly around him. This was not the response he expected from Lan Martak. It was as if this human creature were another inhabiting Lan Martak's body.

"You did well, Lan," said Kiska. The woman's thin fingers stroked his arm and came to rest on his shoulder. He seemed to bathe in the admiration showered upon him by his bitter enemy.

"Thanks. I knew Lirory wasn't able to stand up to me. Now we go after Claybore."

"No, Lan," said the woman. "You need to rest. Lirory almost killed you."

"Killed me?" Lan's laugh sounded harsh to Krek. "That's not possible. I'm immortal." But he did not rush out to seek Claybore. Instead, he sat upon Lirory's throne. Where the gnome had created a green aura, Lan produced a pale red one. He closed his eyes and soaked in the power being generated from inside the throne.

"Lan Martak, we must go rescue friend Inyx and her companion," said Krek. "If you are not attacking Claybore right away, there is time and need."

"There is no *need*," Lan contradicted. "When Lirory died, his spell on them vanished. Go get Inyx and that Ducasien fellow out of their prison. It ought to be easy now."

"You will not accompany me?" the spider asked, more surprised than hurt.

"Do it," snapped Lan. The Voice echoed throughout the chamber. Krek felt infinite sorrow as he obeyed the magical command—sorrow that he obeyed because he had to rather than because he wanted to. Lan Martak's magics took on more and more power and he used them in ways Krek did not approve of.

The spider lumbered out of Lirory's chamber and down the corridor until he found a trough of acid water seeking a lower level. With care, he skirted the trough and the bubbling liquid it held and spiraled downward to the lowest level of Yerrary. There it took Krek only a few minutes to find the excavations and the cell where Lirory Tefize had left the humans to die.

Krek stood and stared into the cell. Inyx slept, Ducasien's arm protectively around her shoulder. The man simply stared at a blank wall. Krek worried that Lan Martak might have been wrong, that it wasn't possible to get the two from within the cell.

"Friend Inyx," the spider said softly. "I have come for you."

Bright blue eyes snapped instantly open. For a fraction of a second, Inyx looked as if she didn't believe this was happening, that she only dreamed of rescue. Then she shoved herself to her feet and dove forward, arms outstretched. Krek caught her between his two front legs and spun her around clumsily.

"Krek! You did it! You rescued us!" she cried.

"Friend Inyx, I have only come for you. It is Lan Martak who has destroyed Lirory and lifted the spell binding you in the cell."

She frowned slightly and then called to Ducasien, "Come on. We've got work to do! Lan's gotten rid of Lirory Tefize."

Ducasien approached more slowly, as if unsure of the spider's intentions.

"He's my friend, Ducasien," Inyx said, laughing and crying at the same time. "I never thought I'd see him again. Oh, do come on! We've got to join Lan."

Ducasien trailed behind the woman and the spider, stopping only to retrieve their weapons where Lirory had cast them aside before imprisoning them. He caught up and handed the weapons to Inyx, who strapped on the sword-belt and made sure the sword rested easy in its sheath.

"I knew he could do it. I told you he could!" Inyx kept saying over and over.

"Friend Inyx," began Krek. Then the spider stopped. How did he tell her that Lan had not specifically rescued her? In point of fact, Lan had refused to aid her. The spell was broken only as a result of Lirory Tefize's defeat, not because Lan had applied himself to the task directly. While the results were the same, Krek's spiderish mind worried over the motives.

"What's bothering you?" Inyx asked.

"Nothing."

"I knew Lan wouldn't let us rot there." Inyx held out her arms and displayed the tiny reddenings from acid water dribbling down onto her flesh. "We weren't in there long enough to get really hungry or thirsty, but another day of the water coming in on our heads might have finished us off. I'm *so* glad he succeeded in breaking the ward spell!"

They made their way up through Yerrary and back to Lirory's chamber. The sight of Kiska k'Adesina brought forth Inyx's sword in a smooth draw. But before the dark-haired woman could launch a killing attack, Lan stopped her with a single command.

The Voice froze her solid.

"What's going on, Lan?" Inyx raged. She fought against his spell and lost. "Why do you allow her to roam freely? Kill her!"

"No," the young mage said. "I need her."

"For what?" cried Inyx.

"Hush," cautioned Ducasien from one side. "There is more to this than you can unearth easily."

Inyx shot him a hot glare, but quieted. Lan released the spell binding her and she stood, holding her sword in hand, ready for a quick thrust.

"Explain this to me, Lan," she said. "Krek is acting strangely. Is there anything wrong between the two of you?"

"I am very busy. Run along and find some food. Rest. Do something. I need to finish going through Lirory's gri-moire. There is a clue in here somewhere as to how I can best use Claybore's legs against him. He doesn't have them yet, and if I recover them first, I can use them."

"Lan!" protested Inyx. But he had turned from her, dismissed her, had not even properly greeted her.

Inyx's anger rose until Krek forcibly restrained her.

"Lan Martak's power is too great to fight," the spider said. "Do as he commands—for the moment. You need food and water. Both you and friend Ducasien do."

Inyx's gaze snapped around and fixed on Krek's huge brown eyes. Although Krek had named Ducasien "friend," he had pointedly failed to do so with Lan.

Hot tears in her eyes, Inyx spun and left Lan without a backward glance. Krek heaved a deep, shuddering sigh and trailed along behind her, wondering if he should ask if such rude behavior formed a new part of human mating rituals that he knew nothing about.

CHAPTER ELEVEN

Claybore shifted slowly on his metallic legs as his hands stroked over his body. The sensation of touch was superb. For so long he had been without arms and hands that he had forgotten the exquisite sense almost entirely.

Damn Terrill and his meddling ways! And damn the Resident of the Pit for giving Terrill the powers he needed for the initial dismemberment! But Claybore gloated now. He had triumphed, after so many centuries. Terrill lay dead— or better than dead—and the Resident of the Pit had lost all power.

Claybore continued stroking himself as he cast forth his scrying spell. Before him as if they were in the same room stood Lan Martak and Kiska k'Adesina. Only Lirory Tefize's ashes remained on the floor, the throne upon which the gnome had once rested now lay inert, dull, more dead than alive.

"So he has defeated you, my friend," mused Claybore. "It is no great surprise. You were overconfident. If he had not dispatched you so easily, I would have done so soon enough."

Claybore studied the scene with some enjoyment. Lirory had thought to keep the upper hand because Claybore didn't know where his legs were hidden. At that Claybore let out a laugh that echoed along the hallways of infinity, rocking from one planet to the next.

His shadow creature had sniffed out those legs in less than an hour—and located the various traps the gnome had laid. While Lirory's magics had been great, Claybore's were far greater. The shadow hound knew no dimension, slipped in and out of rooms and *through* walls and worlds, seeking, sniffing, finding.

"Should I loose you on him yet?" Claybore asked the shadow hound. A dim outline appeared at the mechanical feet. Savage fangs ripped forth and clamped on the metal leg, bending a strut and breaking off a cogged wheel. With a pass of his wondrously alive hand, Claybore sent the shadow hound bouncing away.

The creature flickered insubstantially as it strove to regain its position on this world. The ebony eyes burned with even darker swirls of hatred and the claws on the front feet pawed futilely in the air.

"Think not to turn on me, beast," cautioned Claybore. "I can send you back into nothingness. Just like this!"

The shadow hound let forth with an anguished howl of frustration and pain and . . . vanished.

Claybore waited for a few seconds, then resummoned the hound. Contrite now, it groveled at his feet. Claybore's fleshless mouth opened in a parody of a smile. This was the way it had been in the old days, when his power was unquestioned, when he was able to do as he pleased on any world. A death here and there—who cared? He had been invincible.

Claybore would be again.

"Come along, my little friend," he said to the shadow hound. "I would speak once more with the Resident."

Claybore delighted in seeing his old nemesis captive and

impotent while his own power returned. He reached the lowest levels of Yerrary and made his way through the rubble to the cistern where the Resident dwelled on this world. Claybore gestured for the hound to find a suitable blood offering. Nothing less than the still-living carcass of some animal would animate the Resident of the Pit.

The hound returned, a small rodent clutched in its mouth. The brown furry rat squealed in anguish as the punishing fangs cut through its flesh and sank bone-deep. Claybore motioned for the shadow creature to deliver the offering. The rat fell into the pit, twisting and trying to snap at its attacker.

A droplet of blood from a wound activated the sequence leading to the summoning of the Resident.

"I wished to speak one last time, Resident of the Pit," said Claybore. "When I regain my legs, I will again be in control. Does that bother you?"

"No," came the baleful reply.

"It ought to. You opposed me once and see where it has landed you. Once you were a god. No longer. I brought about your downfall."

"Terrill brought about yours."

"He is no more," snapped Claybore, the ruby lights in the eye sockets flaring forth in hot anger. "Just as you lost all in that battle, so did he."

"Terrill is not dead."

"Terrill is not alive, either," said Claybore. "I defeated him. I defeated you. And I want you to know that your pawn is soon to fall to my queen."

The Resident of the Pit did not reply. Claybore warmed to the telling, his audience unable to flee. Triumph flared within his breast, turned the Kinetic Sphere a soft, pulsating pink, made his entire body come more alive than it had been in a millennium. He gestured wildly, more for the sensation of movement than to emphasize his point. He wanted to gloat and gloat he would!

"You do not deceive me with your subtle workings, Resident. I know that is all you have left in the way of power. A nudge here, a touch there. Martak will fail you."

"He does not consider himself my pawn."

"He's too stupid. Who else would have given him the abilities he has shown? He destroyed Lirory Tefize with hardly any effort. Lirory was a master mage. I say that it was *you*, Resident, who gave Martak the power. Oh, you were cunning about it. Ask Martak and he'd tell you he gained the ability on his own. I know better."

"He is a remarkably adept human."

"He's a remarkably incapable one," countered Claybore. "You chose him, how or why I can't say, but you picked him to be your champion. I have removed him permanently now."

"How so?"

"Don't play coy, Resident. You know." Claybore strutted around, basking in victory and the way his fingers wiggled once again. He built scintillant scuplures in the air, then destroyed them with a sweep of his arm. This was what it meant to again live.

"My powers fade. I am so weak." The voice trailed off.

"You cannot gull me into such an obvious trap. Nor can you convince me Martak isn't your special pet. But k'Adesina is mine and she subverts his power." Claybore perched on the edge of the cistern, metal feet dangling into the pit. Far below stirred the darkness, so similiar to his own shadow hound and yet so different. "Martak uses his magics and the geas I placed on him grows stronger. He and Kiska k'Adesina are bound magically to one another now. She is a dagger placed at his throat. When the proper moment comes, when he cannot help himself, that dagger will sever his arteries!"

"Using others in such a fashion is but one reason why I opposed you then and do so you now."

"It doesn't matter what you oppose or favor now, Resident of the Pit. I allowed k'Adesina to be captured. Even she does not realize how she has been forged into the perfect weapon against Martak. As the bond grows, so does her outward affection for him. But this is only a guise. Her hatred for him will destroy him—and he will be powerless because of my compulsion geas."

"He is no apprentice. He knows the nature of the spell."

"Oh, yes, he might suspect the geas, but he will be completely unable to do anything about it. That is the beauty of my revenge. Martak understands that Kiska will be his destruction and he cannot stop it. He *welcomes* it and hates himself even as he does."

"Why do you tell me this?" Swirls of black moved through equally black space. Only the adept saw such arcane movement. Claybore saw and clacked his jaws together in delight.

"He robbed me of my flesh. Never again will I be able to look as others do. He has stolen my tongue and misuses its power. But I have rejoined arms and torso and head and heart. Before I take possession of my legs and discard these pathetic mechanical limbs, I wanted you to congratulate me."

No response.

"Come, come, Resident. Give me your blessing. I might even free you from the Pillar." Claybore only baited the captive god. Nothing in the universe would persuade him to free the Resident of the Pit from such carefully wrought imprisonment.

"Throughout the eons, you have not changed, Claybore," came the measured words. "Martak will triumph and become more than you ever dreamed. I see the future and it is his."

"You won't share that future," snarled Claybore.

"I will not share his future," agreed the Resident.

"Watch your pet crushed under foot," said Claybore, his

mood lightening again as victory became a heady possibility. "We will do battle. His most impressive spells will fail. I will be victorious. Wait and see."

The Resident of the Pit did not deign to answer.

Claybore pulled his legs over the rim of the pit and laughed once more. His shadow hound shied away at the sound, fearing new punishments. Claybore motioned for the beast to follow. He wended his way back through the excavation and upward to where Lan Martak toiled to find a clue on how to use the pair of legs to his best advantage.

Claybore would not allow the young mage the opportunity to discover that.

"I know where the legs are," Lan Martak said. "I can see them as plainly as if they were in this very room. But how do I *use* them? What gain did Lirory see from obtaining them?"

"Don't fret," said Kiska k'Adesina, her hand stroking over his light-brown hair. "You are a master now. The way will open to you when you least expect it."

Lan turned and looked at the woman. Manic intensity burned within her, no matter how placid her words. He sensed the magics boiling around them and the subtler undercurrents that bound them together. But try as he might, he found no way of separating their destinies, nor did he have an inkling as to why he protected her as he did. He had to believe it was instinct on his part, a hunch that Kiska would be useful in the battle against Claybore.

But this hardly seemed right. Lan shrugged off the worrisome thoughts.

Claybore knew how difficult it was for Lan to slay wantonly. Even Kiska's husband had not been a careless or thoughtless death at his hand. Surepta had murdered Lan's lover, raped and murdered his half-sister, and had driven him from his home world in disgrace. In spite of all that, the death throes Surepta made as Lan had run him through with a sword had not been satisfactory. No amount of suffering had balanced the cosmic scales for what he had done.

Lan had been warned by the Resident of the Pit that revenge would turn to ash in his mouth. It had. There had been no thrill of victory over Surepta, no feeling of justice being served. The death had been just that—a death both necessary and sickening to him.

"You cannot defeat a mage who has such experience, Lan," the woman told him. "Don't try. Give it up."

He wanted to strike out, to silence her. But there was no way. To use the Voice only hardened the ties between them. A sudden use of magic—another fire elemental— might kill Kiska, but he couldn't do that. Not now. The spell died on his lips before being half-formed.

"I will not allow him those legs," he said firmly.

"He can't get to them. Lirory hid them well."

"I can see them," Lan said tiredly. This wore him down— dealing with Kiska. That was another aspect of the spell. Simply dismissing her as annoying, much like a mosquito buzzing about his head, proved as difficult as killing her. "I am sure Claybore is able to, also. After all, they were once a part of him. The bond between leg and body would be strongest for him."

"You are tired. Rest. Relax."

Lan turned from Lirory's grimoires and sat in the slag rock throne. Energies welled up and bolstered his flagging power. He closed his eyes and wondered if the use of a sudden enough spell wouldn't kill Kiska and free him.

He tried and failed.

Lan ignored Kiska's constant negative comments and cast forth his senses throughout all of Yerrary, seeking, probing, examining. With ease he found the chamber cradling the legs. They radiated a glow he thought should be obvious to anyone, then realized he looked not with his eyes but with other magical senses.

Lan rubbed his temples and felt as if he'd burst into tears at any moment. How far he had come. Gone were the simple days of roving through the woods near his home, finding game, living free. Gone, all gone, and in their place came new powers and even weightier burdens and wearisome responsibilities.

"Lan?" came a familiar voice. He opened his eyes and saw Inyx. For reasons he couldn't fathom, the sight of Ducasien standing so close beside her sent him into a rage.

"What is it?" he yelled.

"We came to see if you needed anything," the woman said, her words turning chilly. "I see you are well enough served."

"I am."

Ducasien started to speak. Lan glared at him and the man fell silent, the words jumbled in his throat. This brought a slight sneer to the mage's lips. This was the way to deal with subordinates—do not allow them to speak unless addressed directly.

Power flared within and he liked it.

"Krek says you'll need help when you meet Claybore." The raven-haired woman tossed her head and brushed away strands of the lustrous hair. She had bathed, eaten, and rested. In other times Lan would have found her heartrendingly beautiful. Now she was little more than an annoyance, an interruption—another of his servants.

"The spider is too prissy for his own good," said Lan. "What does he know of the battles to come? They will be ones of magic. There won't be need for insects."

"Insects?" Inyx's eyebrows shot up. She was too shocked to be angry at the man's words. "Is that all he is to you? A bug?"

"You know what I meant. What will happen will be between mages. Claybore and myself. We will fight and I will win."

The throne on which he sat glowed a deeper-hued red

and power suffused his body until he felt invincible. How had he ever thought Claybore his equal? Lan Martak was better, unconquerable!

"Sorry I even mentioned it," Inyx said bitterly. She motioned to Ducasien to accompany her. The man's hand rested on his throat as he tried to speak. Lan's laughter followed them from the room. Yes, this definitely was the way to handle servants.

"You have learned much, Martak," came the formless words inside his head. Lan's attention snapped to the chamber holding the legs, then slowly circuited the vast interior to the mountain kingdom. He found Claybore some distance away, but that meant nothing. Their magics penetrated rock as well as space and time. Whether they were in the same room or worlds apart, this battle would continue until one of them was defeated.

"You will not recover your legs, Claybore."

"What makes you think I want them, worm?" The sorcerer vented a harsh laugh.

"You want them," said Lan. Already he mounted his ward spells, formed his attacks. The throne energized him and gave a support. Although it looked nothing like the power stone he wore around his neck, the material of the throne served the same purpose. From somewhere on this world it focused the flows needed to transcend mere human capacity.

"Of course I do. I lied to see how you would respond. What good will they do you, Martak? Let me take them. Perhaps we can come to an accommodation in this."

"You're trying to bribe me?"

Even as Lan formed the words, he parried a magical bolt that would have wrecked entire cities. He parried and returned a bolt no whit less powerful.

And so went the battle. Each mage probed for the other's weakness. And neither one found the crucial spot for the final thrusting, the most vulnerable point. Lan called more and more on the throne for power—and felt another attraction.

"Kiska," he moaned softly. "Come to me. I need you!"

And Kiska k'Adesina stood beside him while he battled Claybore. Enemies to the death, they held one another like lovers while Lan's spells sizzled and cracked about their heads. With each spell cast, the fatal attraction grew.

Lan knew what Claybore did. The other sorcerer played a waiting game. The stalemate improved his position immensely, because Lan bound himself more and more tightly to Kiska with every passing instant.

"No!" Lan wailed. A brief flash of insight told him he was lost. The ties between Kiska and himself had been forged too strongly. He mentally slipped and allowed Claybore to rob him of the throne. A spell from the gesturing sorcerer caused frost to form. Lan stood and the throne turned to power behind him.

"Where does your power come from now, Martak?" asked Claybore. "You are growing weaker, even weaker. Surrender to my will!"

Lan heard the words, hated the attraction to Kiska k'Adesina—and oddly, grew stronger. Away from Lirory's throne, new and subtly different power surged through his arteries. He discovered untapped reservoirs within that caused the energy derived from the throne to pale in comparison.

"You *have* learned much," congratulated Claybore.

Lan had learned. No compliment came without its barb.

Lan jumped back just as Claybore's shadow hound slashed out at his legs. The beast had sneaked up on him by coming through other dimensions, other worlds. Kiska hanging on one arm, the hound snapping and clawing at his legs, Lan Martak fought as he'd never fought before.

"Begone!" he cried, forming a spell that violated space around the shadow hound. The creature *puffed!* out of existence. Claybore ceased his attack, and Kiska moved from him to hunker down near a low wooden table.

Stunned at the sudden cessation of all battle, Lan reeled and reached out to support himself. He staggered until he found a wall. Head ringing like a bell, sweat pouring from him in rivers, he panted as if he'd finished running a daylong race.

"You won!" came Kiska's words.

But Lan knew that was false. He had not won. He had lost. Claybore played the game skillfully. He had traded the shadow hound for a strengthened geas binding Kiska to Lan. No matter how he tried now, Lan Martak knew he could never allow himself to be separated from Kiska k'Adesina.

What would Claybore's next move be? Lan couldn't tell, but he knew he'd soon enough discover it.

CHAPTER TWELVE

Krek stood to one side watching as Lan Martak battled Claybore. The shadow hound vanished with a *pop!* and the struggles ceased. All that remained in the chamber was the lingering feeling that, while Claybore had left, he had not been defeated.

"You won!" cried Kiska k'Adesina. "To defeat a mage with Claybore's power you must be the greatest who ever lived."

Krek watched carefully as Lan reacted. The play of emotion on the human's face bothered the spider. He knew so little about what actually made Lan Martak what he was. The feeling he had, though, was not good. Lan responded to his bitter enemy's compliments.

"I haven't won," said Lan. "He still seeks his legs—and I do not have them. I must get them. I must!"

Inyx came to stand beside Krek, her hand resting on one of his furry legs.

"What do you think?" she asked.

"He will not listen to anything we say," the spider replied. "But he will listen to her."

"Why?"

"You humans go about things in ways too bizarre to comment upon," said Krek. "I have often wondered at his tastes."

"This is different," insisted Inyx.

Krek said nothing. The dramatic transformation in his friend was not one he liked seeing. The kindness he had witnessed before in Lan Martak now vanished, to be replaced by coldness. The mage was driven by a single-minded determination to destroy Claybore. That wasn't evil. But the changes occurring in Lan Martak were—especially his inability to force Kiska k'Adesina away.

"He doesn't need us," said Ducasien. The man stood close to Inyx and hesitated when he started to put his arm around her waist. Krek saw that the woman was torn between Ducasien and Lan, not willing to commit herself to either one—not fully, not at this moment.

He shared the dark-haired human's confusion.

"He does," said Inyx, but conviction wasn't in her tone. "Ask him."

Inyx glared at Ducasien, then stormed forward and planted her feet firmly in front of Lan.

"What can we do to help you defeat Claybore?" she asked.

The expression on Lan's face caused even Inyx to take a step back. The contempt written there was withering.

"I don't need you," he said. "Your powers are no longer sufficient. Claybore and I fight on a different plane. We battle among the worlds, all along the Cenotaph Road." He smirked when he said, "Only I can defeat him. Not even Terrill was strong enough. I am."

"Leave us," said Kiska, her tone haughty and her expression as contemptuous as Lan's.

"I don't take orders from you, bitch," snapped Inyx. Her dagger seemed to leap into her hand of its own volition and the warrior woman swung without even realizing she made the effort. The blade struck something substantial in midair.

Lan's hand had been raised and his fingers moved in arcane magical patterns.

"Let me kill her," raged Inyx. "She is destroying you. Listen to this bitch's words and Claybore will eat your soul!"

"Claybore doesn't control her," Lan said. "I do. And I want her by my side. I . . . I need her." Sweat popped out on his forehead as he spoke and he began shaking as if he had a palsy.

"Lan Martak," spoke up Krek, "look to yourself. You are the weapon needed to stop Claybore. That much is evident. But you are destroying yourself. Without you, what chance does any of us have?"

"None," the man said. The strain passed and the contempt returned. "You're only a spider. And her, she's not even that." His brown eyes locked on Inyx's cold blue ones.

Inyx spun and stormed off. Ducasien glared at Lan and followed the woman. Krek remained behind, emotionally torn in this matter. The spider felt himself at a crossroads and unsure what road to take from this point into the future.

"You did not say the proper words, Lan Martak," said Krek. "You embarrassed and enraged friend Inyx. That is no way to treat her after her long and loyal—and loving—service."

"Let her go," said Lan. "She can't help me any more."

"And this lumpy female can?" Krek pointed to Kiska.

Lan said nothing, but the sweat began beading on his forehead once again. The strain he endured had to be tremendous, but his words did nothing to escape the geas.

"She can," Lan Martak said.

"She will destroy you. She *is* destroying you. She is Claybore's pawn and nothing more. How does she treat you? Why do you allow her to know your strategies, your tactics? If she means so much, place her in safety—somewhere far away."

"No!"

"Lan Martak, you are in danger from her."

"Shut up, you miserable web-hanger. I have more important things to do. I have to find Claybore. Defeat him. He...he can't recover his legs. And I know where they are. But using them—how do I use them for my own gain?"

"There are things worse than being conquered by Claybore," said Krek. "Loss of your own self-esteem is one."

"Get out of here. Let me alone!"

Krek saw that Lan's temper rose to a dangerous level. The mage's fingers twitched and fat blue sparks jumped from one tip to the other. A fiery blast and Krek would be set afire. Krek didn't know if there was any fate he feared more, unless it was drowning—or losing the friend who had been Lan Martak.

"When you need help, you can find me with friends Inyx and Ducasien."

Krek lumbered out of the chamber, leaving Lan and Kiska to their work poring over the grimoires left by Lirory Tefize. Krek had no doubt that, locked within one of those magical tomes, lay the secret of how to use Claybore's legs against him. He also knew that the mere act of allowing Kiska k'Adesina to watch the search provided Claybore with inestimable advantage. She still worked for the disembodied sorcerer.

In the hallway Krek overtook Inyx and Ducasien.

"Where do you go, friend Inyx?" the spider asked.

"I don't know," she said, close to tears. "He's never been this way before. I've been with him when he's bone-tired, half-dead, pushed far beyond the limits of human endurance, and never has Lan acted that way toward me."

"Forget him, Inyx. Come with me. We can walk the Road together. This isn't the life for you," Ducasien said earnestly. "What does it matter if Claybore conquers or not? Will things change so much? We can find a backwater world, peaceful, away from the centers of power. He'd never bother us there."

Krek saw Inyx wavering. The offer tempted her greatly. And it appealed to the spider, also. This continual battling across worlds took its toll on him. He wanted nothing more than to return to his web and his mate, even if dear Klawn might try to eat him.

"I feel friend Ducasien has made a good case for our doing just as he recommends," said Krek. "Lan Martak is obsessed with victory over Claybore. Is victory such a needful thing?"

Inyx stared at the spider and slowly shook her head.

"Lan knows more than we do. He senses the evil Claybore brings more clearly than anyone else can. And we've got to support him. I don't know what's gotten into him, but we can't just walk out on him. Not when he needs us more than ever."

"We have been through much with him," agreed Krek. "The war for the iron tongue resting within his mouth was a costly one." The arachnid stopped speaking for a moment, then added, "Is it possible he is infected by Claybore's spirit through that tongue?"

"Who can say? When Lan first used it, he claimed he was more powerful. I think his behavior is sparked by something more than his own abilities. Perhaps it *is* the tongue's doing."

"He certainly isn't doing it to protect you," said Ducasien.

"Danger has been at our side ever since we've been together," Inyx said. She smiled up at Krek. "He rescued me from the whiteness between worlds. Another would have left me."

"I wouldn't have," said Ducasien.

"Friend Ducasien, you would have been unable to reach her," said Krek. "The magics involved were the most complex Claybore was capable of invoking. Only a mage of Lan Martak's caliber could have been successful."

"I'd have died trying," Ducasien maintained.

"Thank you," said Inyx. "I appreciate that. But Lan *did* rescue me. And not just that one time. We've been through much. Turning away now is difficult, no matter how he acts."

"Let us go and ponder this further," suggested Krek. "Another course of action might suggest itself." The spider and Inyx started off, Ducasien remaining behind. Krek stopped and twisted in an inhuman fashion to look under and behind his huge body. "Please come with us, friend Ducasien. Your experience will be most valuable."

Ducasien hesitated, then joined the pair. This time Inyx did not flinch away when Ducasien put his arm around her shoulders. Her own arm circled his waist and off they went, talking in low, confidential tones of what their best strategy might be.

"It's got to be here. It must be!" raged Lan Martak. Anger rose and he clapped hands together to form a thunderbolt that almost deafened Kiska k'Adesina. She kept her hands over ears until it was obvious the mage's wrath had abated slightly.

"Lirory kept his diaries in code," she said. "The code might take months to decipher."

"I've read his books," said Lan in disgust. "The code depended on a simple magical combination obvious to even an apprentice. The information is not written down."

"Perhaps he carried it within his head," she said.

"I can't dismiss that as a possibility," Lan said. He stalked back and forth across the room, eyes fixed on the floor in front of him. "The legs are near but I won't go after them until I have a way of *using* them. What did Lirory have in mind for them?"

"If Claybore knows where his legs are, also, why hasn't he already tried to retrieve them?" The brunette gingerly sat on the single block remaining of Lirory Tefize's throne. The power that had welled up and bathed both the gnome and Lan Martak did not come to her. She didn't know whether to be miffed or relieved.

"Lirory protected them, of that I'm sure. Claybore is cautious. I have already robbed him of his skin and his tongue. To lose his legs would be a blow second to none. He dares not make a mistake now."

"He is close to dominance on all the worlds along the Road," said Kiska.

"Claybore is far from it," Lan contradicted. "The last encounter proves that. I am the stumbling block on his path. His grey legions might swarm and physically seize world after world, but without his magic to back them, they are nothing. I can defeat them all with a wave of my hand."

To demonstrate Lan lifted his arm and fire flickered from his fingertips. Then alternate fingertips froze solid while the others blazed with wild witchfire. He jerked his hand in a small circle and sent a ball of light burning through the rock vault of Lirory's chamber and up through the mountain until it ripped apart the sky itself.

"You are a mighty mage," said Kiska. Even as she spoke, the loathing for what she did built within her. The woman struggled to keep from puking. In a dim fashion she understood Claybore used her against Martak, but this role did not suit her well. Playing the toady to the man who had killed her husband revolted her. She would be more at home driving a barbed shaft into Martak's guts, then twisting until the entrails billowed forth.

How long would they be, she wondered. Long enough to string around the room? Would this appease her intense hatred for the man? Kiska k'Adesina wanted to find out. It might even be possible to rip his intestines from his belly and let him linger.

Martak had killed her husband with a single sword thrust. His own death would not be so easy.

Damn Claybore for what he did to her! The geas binding Martak bound her, as well.

Lan turned and looked at her, his expression softening. She made a small gesture beckoning him to her side. To her disgust he came like a lovesick puppy dog.

"I need you so," Lan said. "To think I tried to kill you so many times. That's all so unreal to me. A nightmare."

"You are the greatest man in all the universe," she whispered. Kiska longed for him to be closer, to take her in his arms, to make love to her. And then, at the precise moment of climax, she would drive a dagger into his back. Then would her revenge be sweet.

"The others don't understand the strain I am under. Krek demands attention all the time. He . . . he's not human. He can't understand what it's like seeing evil such as Claybore's loose in the world."

"And your Inyx?" Kiska almost hissed. What she'd do to that bitch made her revenge on Lan Martak seem pale in comparison. There would be mismatings with a dozen ferocious animals on a hundred barbaric worlds before she allowed Inyx to die.

"I don't know what's got into her. She seems so distant now. We had a rapport I can't explain. Our thoughts were as one—but that was before we came onto this world."

"The fog?" suggested Kiska.

"That might have something to do with it. Or it might be something else." Bitterness came to Lan Martak.

"Ducasien," Kiska said, striking the soft spot in Martak's heart. She sensed his jealousy of the man from Inyx's home world and played on it. His anguish thrilled her even if she did not allow it to be mirrored on her face.

"What does she see in him?" he wondered aloud.

"There is definite love for him," goaded Kiska. "The pair of them have been intimate."

The man's expression told her she traveled unsafe territory. No matter how potent Claybore's magical workings, the power over Lan Martak was not complete.

"She loves me."

"Who couldn't?" asked Kiska, stroking Lan's cheek. The man pulled away, hesitated, turned back to her. Every use of magic on his part strengthened the spell binding the two of them together. Kiska saw that Lan became less and less aware of Claybore's intrusion in this matter, another manifestation of the spell.

Even she found it increasingly difficult to remember the few things Claybore had told her before sending her forth. A dagger at the enemy's back, Claybore had said. A chance for revenge, he'd said. Kiska k'Adesina hadn't questioned her master; she was too good a soldier for that. She did not care for this form of warfare, but if it gained her ends, so be it.

Lan Martak would die at her hand. Claybore had promised that. She held on grimly to that single thought.

"The legs," Lan said suddenly. "Why can't I grasp their importance, their use?"

"Rest, my darling," Kiska said, sickened by her honeyed words. "Rest and it will all come to you. You overwork yourself. Tired, you can't hope to win. Rest, sleep, sleep, yes, sleep."

She cradled his head and held it close. Muscles in her upper arms twitched spasmodically as she fought down the urge to place one hand on the man's chin and another on the top of his head and jerk as hard as she could. That might break his neck.

It might also fail.

Her time would come. Soon. Claybore promised it. Soon.

CHAPTER THIRTEEN

The world exploded around Lan Martak, stars orbiting wildly about his head, the very planet tipping and gyrating and sending him to his knees. The walls of the pyramid-shaped stone chamber first cracked and then turned to powder. The floor beneath his feet became transparent and he hung suspended over a bottomless pit.

And wind— Wind seared his flesh, threatening to strip his bones clean. Squinting, arm up to protect his face, he looked into the gale-force wind and saw an all too familiar figure: Claybore.

The chalk-white skull showed thin fracture lines—and this gave Lan hope. He had put those cracks in Claybore's skull. And he could do more, ever so much more.

"This is silly, Claybore," he said, fighting to keep his face covered. "You attack with only wind?"

"Surely a man of your vast ability recognizes an air elemental when you encounter one," the other mage said with studied politeness. "If you don't like it, I'll stop it. Now!"

The sorcerer's newly attached arms rose and formed a steeple over the skull.

Lan dropped into the pit.

He felt his stomach jerk and the air whistling around him in a new direction. The wind he could tolerate. To allow Claybore to cast him downward meant only death. With a surge of effort, he formed a new floor under his left foot. A solid patch took shape under his right and stopped his insane fall. Slowly, the hardness spread, merged with other spots, rose.

He again faced Claybore, the floor substantial once again.

"Very good," said Claybore. "The illusion is not a common one. You defeated it nicely. Your skill has grown to rival mine."

Lan did not reply with words. He sent his own air elemental shrieking mindlessly for Claybore's body. He hoped to catch the sorcerer off balance and knock him to the floor. With any luck the skull might smash into the stone and crack further.

Luck was not with him. Claybore easily withstood the writhing, screaming puff of air and dismissed it with the wave of a hand. Lan realized then how important those arms and hands were to Claybore. They not only augumented his power, they gave him command over a new set of spells.

"Surrender!" Lan said, using the Voice. The vibrancy of the tongue within his mouth caused the onset of a headache unlike any he had felt. He immediately stopped and the shooting pain diminished and finally went away entirely.

"You cannot use my tongue against me like that, fool," said Claybore, now turning to his usual manner. All pretense of politeness stopped. "I can give you undreamed of powers. You still learn. I know!" The jaws of the skull clattered together emphasizing the words that were not spoken but were still heard.

"You can give me nothing, Claybore. You seek too much power. You must be destroyed."

"Why try?" asked Claybore, his tone curious. "You oppose me, but why? What is it to you? There isn't the hard core within you to make power your goal."

"I don't want dominance over others," said Lan. "I want freedom from that power. You won't impose your will on me or anyone else."

"And you don't want to impose your will on others?" asked Claybore, as if genuinely surprised at finding a fact he had not ever considered to have existed.

Lan Martak spun about, his fingers strewing sparks. The powdery ruins of Lirory Tefize's chamber snapped back into their original form.

"Your illusions fail you, Claybore."

"Do they?" the sorcerer asked softly. "You find the simple ones. The more complex ones might amaze you—had you the wit to see them."

Lan shifted uneasily at those words. Something gnawed at the corners of his mind, as if Claybore had given him a crucial clue to unlocking the dismembered mage's power. He groped for the clue and failed to find it.

"Lan?" came a hesitant voice. "Are you all right? You look strained."

He blinked and lost sight of Claybore, his physical eyes now doing the "seeing" for his mind. Kiska k'Adesina stood before him, the expression on her face a mixture of emotions he couldn't put into words. Whatever he read there, true caring was not present.

"I'm fine," he said. "Claybore started an attack. Didn't you see what he did?"

The woman shook her head, a brown shimmer of hair circling her face. She pushed a vagrant strand back and simply stared at him.

He heaved a sigh. The visions Claybore sent were designed strictly for him. The battle they fought was a personal one and need not involve others—unless drawing others into the conflict aided one of them. Lan tried to figure out

how best to use Kiska against Claybore and failed. The
mage had made no mention whatsoever about her capture;
it was as if this was a problem belonging to Lirory and since
the gnome had perished, the matter was closed.

"It won't be long before we have one last meeting," said
Lan. "The time is drawing close. I sense the powers mounting all around and . . . and I can't control them." The in-
security of his position troubled him strangely. Never before
had he worried over this to such an extent. He held more
power than any mage except Claybore and now he hesitated,
now he doubted himself.

"You tire so easily," said Kiska. "You do need to rest.
Don't let Claybore force you into a battle you can't win."

"What's it to you?" Lan flared. "You are his chief commandant now that Silvain is gone. You should be thinking
of his welfare, not mine. Or is that the way it really is? Are
you thinking of Claybore's victory? Is this part of it?"

"Lan, how can you say that?" Kiska's words soothed
him enough that the edge of anger left. Only confusion
remained. He turned from her to go to the table holding
Lirory's grimoires. Placing both hands on the table, Lan
leaned forward, head down and eyes closed tightly.

It was growing harder to concentrate.

"Nothing seems right to me anymore. Claybore's words
bother me."

"He is your enemy."

"He seems more and more like me. Or I'm adopting his
philosophy." That idea made Lan even more uneasy. If
Claybore weren't changing, then *he* had to be the one becoming more like the disembodied sorcerer. They fought—
but were their motives so different now?

He started to speak and found it impossible. Lan's eyes
flashed open and he saw the room had again turned transparent. The slightest movement caused him pain; all he knew
as the gut-twisting agony lodged deep within him was that

he had failed. Self-pitying, he had let down his guard and now all was lost.

He waited for Kiska to say something, to chastise or to praise. The words never came. Lan retraced the course of their conversation and came once more to the point of her being Claybore's chief architect of destruction on a dozen worlds—Claybore's pawn.

Just as he was Claybore's pawn.

From deep within boiled the power that had once been his and that Claybore had cunningly buried with his spells. The pain in arms and legs lingered, but Lan forced movement into them. He straightened and found the dancing light mote that had become his constant companion. The light mote appeared indistinct, blurred, far away. He coaxed it closer and set it to blazing like a million stars.

Pain dissolved from his body like snow melts in the morning sun. The walls of the room became translucent, then opaque. He cast a spell to insure that Claybore would never again be able to confuse his senses with such conjurings again.

"Claybore," he said softly. "This is one battle that will be fought to the bitter end. One or the other of us will not survive it. We cannot continue together in the same universe, not like this. One of us will perish."

Ghostly, mocking laughter greeted him.

"We are immortal, you and I. Survive this petty difference of opinion? Of course we will. Both of us. The real question you ought to ask is the loser's condition."

"If I have to, I'll scatter your body back along the Road. Terrill did it once. I can do it, also."

Laughter. And pain.

Lan doubled over as his insides ripped apart. For a moment he forgot this was a duel of magics. Ruled only by the physical, he sensed his life force slipping away, his body being torn asunder. He reached once more for the depths of his power and came away empty. This attack, as simple as it was, had defeated him.

Lan Martak felt life draining from him.

And then the flow stopped. Seizing the opportunity, he summoned forth his light mote. The light familiar entered and suffused through his body, leaving him weak but in control once more. The memory of pain and the need to avoid further anguish allowed him to fend off Claybore's renewed attack. The other mage sensed his spells failing and hurled more and more potent, less and less subtle ones at Lan.

They failed. And Lan found conjurings of his own that he hadn't realized he knew to cast against Claybore.

"Pressure," he muttered. "Pressure unlike anything you have ever felt!"

Claybore let out a scream that almost deafened Lan. The spell compressed the sides of Claybore's skull, producing more and deeper cracks. The jaw came unhinged and clattered to the floor.

"And more," said Lan, the power his once again. He didn't understand why the sudden change had occurred within him. He accepted and used it. To defeat Claybore now meant freedom all along the Cenotaph Road, for him and for Inyx and Krek and everyone else. The conquering grey legions Claybore commanded would soon fall into disarray without their mage-general.

The spell crushed down on Claybore's body, compressing the torso and breaking the reattached arms. Lan almost cried aloud in triumph when he saw the Kinetic Sphere— Claybore's heart—slowly being squeezed from the chest cavity. Victory was within his grasp. And still the power flowed to him.

"This can't be," moaned Claybore. "It *won't* be!"

Lan staggered as his spells rebounded and found... nothingness. Claybore had vanished from between the anvils of his magic.

"Where did you go?" he cried out. "Let's finish this now, once and for all!"

Only deathly silence greeted him. He had been close, so very, very close and now victory had been stolen from him. Claybore had eluded him at the last possible instant. Lan sent his dancing light mote forth to seek out Claybore. Long minutes passed and the mote reported no trace of the other sorcerer. Disheartened, Lan propped himself against a table and wondered how he might find Claybore, who had obviously fled this world and traveled the Road.

As he worked out this problem, a new one occurred to him. He sensed another powerful presence on this world, in Yerrary.

"Lirory's dead," he said aloud.

"Lan, you look so drawn. What's happened?" Kiska k'Adesina's concern struck him as hollow and a lie. She cared nothing for him. But even as he thought this, other emotions surfaced and his view toward her softened.

"Claybore has left Yerrary—even this world. I can't track him down. I'll have to follow him to other places, but there's a power emanating from down below I had not felt before. Or rather, I have felt it before."

"You're not making sense."

Lan realized the woman was right. His confusion centered on the familiarity of that power center and the impossibility of it. The other time when he had flagged in battle with Lirory and Claybore, this source had opened to him with the same feeling of elusive recognition. What it was stayed just beyond his grasp, yet he knew it.

"Stay here," he said to the woman. "I've got to explore and see if I can't get some answers."

"I'm coming with you," Kiska declared.

Lan started to protest but didn't find it within him to tell her no. He motioned and she hurried along, matching his long strides as he found all the right corridors and down ramps to take him into the newer parts of Yerrary still being dug out from the living bedrock of the planet. The excavations were abandoned and he had to step over piles of rock and go around large boulders, but his stride was sure and his destination plain in his mind. The place he sought glowed with a dark power and drew him like a magnet pulls iron.

"Where are we going?" Kiska asked him.

He didn't answer. He pushed aside rock, jumped back as the poorly buttressed roof sent down a shower of small stones and dust, and kept on until he came to the chamber Claybore had visited. Traces of the other mage lingered; Lan sensed the magical residues indicating physical presence. Whatever lay within this room was important enough to demand that Claybore actually be here.

"What's this cistern?" asked Kiska, going up to the low rock wall and cautiously peering down into the blackness. She shivered and looked away. "I don't like it, whatever it's for."

"I've seen it before. On my home world." Lan experienced a dizziness as sensations rushed in on him.

"It's only a well."

"It's more," he said. Lan looked around the room and saw no sign of life. For a crazy instant he considered shoving Kiska into the pit to satisfy the blood urges of the entity living at its bottom—if the pit had a true physical bottom. "Wait here. I'll return in a few minutes," he said.

Kiska started to follow, but a minor spell rooted her to the spot, her muscles frozen. Lan Martak walked like one still asleep as he traced his way through the diggings and came to a chamber with pipes and vats. His mind had slipped into a curious fugue state, not fully rational and yet knowing what to do. None dared stand in his way now, even if his movements appeared mechanical, alien.

He hardly glanced around the huge room, even though he had never seen it before. Streams of burning water poured down the stone walls all around as pipes leaked and vats were decanted. The troughs spiraling down from above were filled to their rims with the acid water that continually poured from the outer sky.

Hopping out to see who invaded his domain came the toadlike Eckalt.

"What is it?" the creature demanded. "My time is precious. You interrupt important work. There's water to be . . . aieee!"

Lan made a quick pass with his hand and stifled the toad-being's words. Still as if he walked in a daze, Lan returned to the chamber containing the cistern. Eckalt half-hopped, half was dragged by the spell Lan had cast. Without allowing the being another word, Lan physically picked up Eckalt and dropped him into the pit.

Amid the curtains of blackness came a stirring.

The Resident of the Pit spoke.

"Lan Martak, we meet once again. It has been a considerable time for you and only a fraction of a second for me."

"Resident of the Pit," he said unsteadily, "did you aid me in my duel with Claybore?"

"The questions most important are those least asked. For the true question, look into your own soul and study what you find. But perhaps those answers are the hardest to accept."

"You did help me?"

"I gave you nothing but the vision of what powers you truly commanded."

"What is this?" asked Kiska. "There're things moving down inside the well, but I can't make them out. Is this a ghost?"

Lan ignored her, as did the Resident.

"If you only revealed what was already inside of me, why can't I defeat Claybore? Can I?"

"Claybore is a cunning mage and a powerful one. He

has claimed to be immortal."

"He said I was immortal, also."

"Lan Martak, many make the claim. Few actually are. And those select few are the damned."

Lan went cold inside.

"Explain, Resident of the Pit. What do you mean by that?"

"Your destiny lies not on this world but on another."

"Where Claybore retreated?"

The Resident didn't answer directly. The obliqueness troubled Lan more than prediction of complete failure would have.

"Decisions are never easy. The past must be laid to rest before the future can be born."

"What are you telling me? Will I defeat Claybore? If he's immortal, I can't kill him."

"You, too, are immortal."

Lan's mind raced. The wording answered the question. Claybore hadn't lied about this. Lan looked down at his body as if seeing something new. Immortal? The idea was hard to accept.

"I can't die?"

"Physical death is not your primary concern," said the Resident of the Pit.

"Claybore is," said Lan. "I need to find him. Give me the powers I need to find and defeat him."

"*Give* you the powers?" came the answer after a long pause, as if this astounded the entity within the well. Lan couldn't tell if it was scorn or amusement locked within this answer.

"He's still more powerful than I am. Give me what I need to destroy him."

"Claybore imprisoned me. I cannot *give* you power to destroy him. That is one condition of my servitude."

"Then tell me where I can find him. You're a deity. You can do that much. You once said your being spread across all space and time. You have to be able to find him."

"For millennia I have been trapped and virtually powerless. All I could do was keep shifting Claybore's parts about to keep him from recovering them, but he has grown far too strong for that ploy now. Other weapons must be used."

"Tell me!" cried Lan, frustrated.

"Use your own instincts. Consider Claybore and his immediate goal. Would he abandon his legs?" The voice of the Resident faded and the stirrings in the shadowy depths of the well began to subside.

But Lan hardly noticed. He came out of his inner fog and smiled when the answer came to him.

"Claybore's legs are still here. They're locked in a chamber over there." He pointed at a solid rock wall.

"Where?" asked Kiska eagerly.

"Some miles off through solid rock, but there, still there. No, Claybore wouldn't abandon them. He needs those legs. And he didn't flee when I began to triumph over him. He only hid. He's around somewhere. He's got to be!"

Lan again sent out his light mote and again it returned without discovering Claybore's hiding place. Frustrated, he sat on the rim of the well and thought even harder, his mind once more beginning to really function. Nothing was wrong with his logic. Claybore had simply outsmarted him, made better use of the magics at his command.

Lan's fingers traced out a simple triangle in the air in front of him. He began the chant to produce a scrying spell he'd found in Lirory's grimoire. At first the air remained calm and only the three-sided frame burned with activity. Then Lan found the right combinations of minor spells and a picture formed within the perimeter.

"He *is* still within Yerrary!" he said. The familiar skull loomed starkly and then winked out. But Claybore's defeating the magic didn't matter. He had found out the sorcerer hid. That information alone made the effort worthwhile.

"You have become his equal," said Kiska.

The woman sat beside him on the rim, her leg brushing against his. Her hand reached out hesitantly, lightly brushed his, then moved upward to undo the fastenings on his tunic. Lan watched in silence, his heart feeling as if it would leap from his breast.

"I want you," Kiska said softly. Her words came out choked with emotion.

Lan started to brush her off, to push on and complete what he saw as his mission—to destroy Claybore's legs. But welling up from deep within came emotions Lan couldn't control.

"And I want you," he said in a weak voice. Their lips met, crushed together passionately. Then their bodies pressed tightly and they slipped to the cold rock floor. Neither noticed, neither minded as they slowly twined and untwined, each movement carrying them closer to their mutual goal.

Lan looked down into Kiska's desire-wracked face and felt the dizzy confusion of emotions vying for supremacy. She was his most hated enemy, the woman sworn to kill him, and now he made love to her. He saw the same contradictions mirrored in her face even as he moved above her, his hips swinging and hers lifting upward.

Faster and faster they moved together until the world burst around them.

Lan sank forward, his arms circling Kiska's thin body. The woman's brown eyes blazed with unholy glee as she gazed past his shoulder and at the silent Inyx standing in the entryway, her face pale and her hands shaking. Inyx had witnessed it all and Kiska took sadistic pleasure in knowing it.

Without a word, Inyx turned and walked off. Her once confident stride now faltered and she stumbled twice within Kiska k'Adesina's sight.

Kiska immediately turned her attention back to Lan Martak, began doing small things, intimate things, and soon enough they were again passionately engaged.

Kiska k'Adesina's revenge had been fed but not sated. That would come. Claybore had promised her that it would come. Soon.

CHAPTER FOURTEEN

"The spells. They are incredible. Since speaking with the Resident of the Pit, I'm able to see what Lirory meant rather than what he wrote." Lan Martak hunched over the table creaking under the weight of Lirory's grimoires. The pages now burned with runic writings. The man's eyes scanned the arcane words with practiced ease.

"Did this Resident creature give you this extra ability?" asked Kiska k'Adesina.

"I don't know. I don't think so, but simply being near such power as he commands might have released reservoirs inside me I hadn't known existed."

"You're the greatest mage to ever walk the Road," she cooed.

Lan smiled broadly at the praise. He felt nothing hollow in it at all. The spell had progressed too far for that. Lan saw only love and adoration—and felt only love and adoration for Kiska.

"This book is a record of Lirory's travels along the Road seeking out Claybore's parts. He used a spell to locate the arms and draw them back to the tunnel where he placed them in special boxes. When he had them safely in place, he collapsed the tunnel and left them there for almost forty Yerrary years."

"What is this spell? Can you use it?"

"I know the spell now as well as Lirory, but there's no need for it. The arms are once more connected to Claybore's torso."

"But the legs?" Kiska pressed.

"I can sense their location without Lirory's spell." Lan turned and perched on the edge of the table, one leg idly swinging, his mind lost in the intricacy of the gnome's ancient lore. "Lirory had a reason for collecting the parts."

"He wanted to blackmail Claybore."

"That wasn't it. He had a use for them. I know it. Lirory had pretensions of being ruler of everything along the Road himself. There was some spell, some conjuration, requiring those parts that would give him the power he sought."

"He had control of Yerrary. What more could a gnome want?"

"You underestimate him. These grimoires show he was a powerful mage. And my duel with him proved that. He had the ability to rule—certainly as beneficently as Claybore," Lan added with a hint of sarcasm. "But how did he plan to use the legs? Those seem to be the key to Lirory's entire plan. The arms were important, but the legs are the cornerstone of his conquest."

Lan felt the answer dancing at the edges of his mind, just as his light mote bobbed to and fro. He smiled a bit and let the mote come closer. The mage saw the surface of his familiar ripple with pride at the attention he gave it. Before he had conjured this fine companion, it had been nothing—nothingness. Now it lived and took on an existence finer than anything else in the universe.

Lan basked in its admiration, its need to please him. And why shouldn't it try to give him his every desire? He was more than human now. He was an immortal!

"Lan?" came the cautious, questioning voice. "You look . . . different."

"Different?" he said. "Yes, I am. Ever since I spoke with the Resident, I have been stronger."

Lan Martak felt the power growing within. What power that was he couldn't put into words, nor did he desire to try. But he was filled with an energy that ran without limit. Never again would he become drained over the simplest of spells.

He let fire dance from finger to finger and smirked. Once this had been the only spell he knew. Now it was the most trivial of thousands. He could send forth lightning blasts that tore apart mountains. All of Yerrary might split asunder, should he ever feel the whim. The entire world could be sent spinning crazily into its sun if he summoned the proper elementals.

Nothing was beyond his power now. Even Claybore acknowledged that. And Claybore would soon be defeated. Even if the disembodied sorcerer couldn't be killed, he could be strewn once more along the Road. And he'd soon enough suffer that fate. Lan Martak would do what Terrill had failed to do, too. Stopping Claybore so that he never again menaced a single solitary soul burned as Lan's only goal.

"You look odd," said Kiska.

"Odd?" Anger flared irrationally. "I am not odd. Never say such a thing."

Kiska cringed at his wrath. And this was as it should be. He was more than a mere human now. Not only was he immortal, he held the reins of the universe in his hand. A single flick of those reins and empires fell. Lan Martak. Invincible!

"I meant nothing by it, Master."

"Master?" he said, anger gone and replaced with confusion. He hardly knew what to do or say anymore. He flew into rages with no good reason. And Kiska k'Adesina spoke the title in both fear and veneration. He wanted neither.

Or did he? The taste of power was sweet. Almost too sweet.

Kiska dropped to her knees and lowered her gaze to the floor.

"Get up," he said irritably. "Don't worship me. I'm no god. I'm not even a king and don't want to be." Lan spoke the words, but feelings quivered within that told him he wasn't being totally truthful. Success had rammed its barb in his psyche and wouldn't easily dislodge.

"Sorry," she said. "I only meant to say you seem to be . . . more. More than you were."

"I am." Like a blazing star blossoming in the night sky, revelation came to him. "I have powers undreamed of. And I know."

"What, Master?"

"I can shift from world to world without a cenotaph. And I can do it without using Claybore's Kinetic Sphere, also." He walked around the chamber, his eyes glazed. "It's so obvious. The chant, the spells, the weavings of power. It's all so clear to me."

He began the chant and simply winked out of existence. Kiska roared in rage and raced forward, hands groping to find him.

"Come back!" she shrieked. "You can't leave me like this. You can't do it, damn your eyes!"

A tiny pop! betrayed his return. Lan sat on Lirory's work table, laughing.

"So simple. I was again atop Mt. Tartanius. The shrine to Abasi-Abi stands and his son still tends it. I did not speak to him. I noted his presence and left before he took heed."

Lan experienced a dizziness that quickly passed. He knew of powers and places of which even Claybore was ignorant. To defeat the other sorcerer would be child's play. So easy, so very easy. Lan's laughter filled the chamber and echoed along the phosphorescent moss-illuminated corridors of Yerrary.

* * *

Krek slumped into a brown heap on one side of Inyx's room. Broit Heresler and Ducasien spoke softly, not wishing to disturb either the woman's or the spider's foul mood.

Inyx rose and went to sit beside Krek. She leaned against the hard throax and placed her head back so that she stared up at the ceiling. The lack of shadows within the room due to the moss growing on walls and ceiling had bothered her at first. No shadows, no texture. The light softly thrust its way everywhere, causing everything to look soft and bloated.

She shook herself free of such thinking. She avoided the real issue by occupying her mind with trivial things.

"Krek," she said. "What are we going to do?"

"About what, friend Inyx?" he asked.

"You know what I'm talking about. Lan. He's so different. Look at the way he allows Kiska k'Adesina to hang around his neck all the time. Not so long ago she was trying to kill him. Now they . . . they—" She bit off the words as tears rolled unashamedly down her cheeks. Inyx had told no one what she had seen down in the Resident of the Pit's chamber. It had hurt her too badly.

"You leak water from your eyes. I find it distressing when you do that. Almost as distressing as when I do it."

"Can't help it," she said peevishly, wiping away the tears. It did no good. More formed.

"You feel betrayed, also. What is it you saw when you went to find him?"

"Nothing, Krek. Forget it." The woman crossed her arms over her breasts and began squeezing down powerfully on her own upper arms. Inyx felt bruises forming and didn't care. Maybe pain would erase the sight of Lan and Kiska making love.

If he had raped the woman, Inyx could have accepted that. But this had been no rape. It was a mutual lovemaking, mutually initiated, mutually enjoyed.

"You saw them together. I witnessed the peculiar human

mating rituals starting. Consummation occurred and you saw it." The spider spoke in an offhand way, as if it didn't make any difference to him. "He has betrayed you just as he did me."

"That was in the heat of battle, Krek. He sent a spell of some sort to get you out of danger. He didn't mean for you to permanently leave him alone—just then."

"Nor did he mean for you to discover him with Kiska. He just wanted you to leave him alone, just then."

"Quit mocking me, damn you!" Inyx raged. She started to get up but a pair of hairy legs trapped and held her. She struggled and saw her efforts weren't availing her anything. Krek was too strong.

"He was our friend once. Will he be again?" the arachnid asked. Before Inyx could answer, Krek went on. "I feel the powers he gains are turning him into someone other than the Lan Martak we knew. The goodness within has been hidden by a darker side. Does power always corrupt? I made a fine Webmaster and did not allow the position to sway my thinking. Why is he so different?"

"He's the man who rescued me when Claybore abandoned me between worlds. I lost count how many times he's risked his life to save you."

"We have done likewise for him."

"Of course we have. And . . . and I love him." Inyx's words were tiny, almost inaudible. She remembered the first shock when she realized there might be a man in her life other than her long-dead husband Reinhardt. Inyx's shock grew when she and Lan made love and found they shared more than bodies. Their minds met and merged in ways she still found frightening and wonderful. His burgeoning power had forced this link and it had been something she wanted, needed. A warrior had to remain aloof. Becoming too friendly with another only caused intensified feelings of loss when the companion was killed. And Lan had shown her that this was totally wrong.

They were closer than man and woman. They were more than one, they were more than two, they were transcendent together.

"And he chooses her over me," Inyx said self-pityingly.

"I sense magic, as you well know," lectured Krek. "You mentioned it. I believe Lan Martak has himself some inkling of the problem. Claybore has set a geas of subtle and cunning power on him. It must have something to do with Kiska k'Adesina."

"You think this is Claybore's doing?" The hope rising within couldn't be held down. Inyx *wanted* to believe the spider.

"It is a more plausible explanation." Krek fell silent for a moment, then added, "Unless he has indeed become corrupted by the power he wields. I have seen it happen in the Web, of course. A hatchling is promoted too rapidly and assumes great duties of importance."

"What?" The woman was confused at how Krek had jumped from Lan to spiderish politics.

"They think respect is due the position rather the individual in that authority spot. Any order they give, no matter how absurd, must therefore be a good one. A sorry state. They become bloated with their own self-importance."

"What happens then?"

"We eat them."

Inyx shivered. Krek's logical thought processes never failed to give her a pang of cold, gut-clutching fear. He spoke so easily of devouring his comrades.

"You think this is the way to handle Lan?" she asked.

"No. Lan Martak is too powerful. He would fry us long before such a course could be carried out. Or drown me. No, he would set fire to me. That is a hideously favorite spell with him." The huge body quaked at the very idea of being turned into a torch.

"What are we to do? I won't give him up. Not to the likes of *her*."

The spider said nothing.

Inyx didn't have any good answer to her own question, either. The best they could do for the moment was sit, wait, and then seize whatever opportunity presented itself. That waiting would be the most difficult she'd ever done, but it had to be done.

The woman turned and looked at Ducasien and experienced even more confusion. What exactly was it she wanted?

There seemed no easy answer.

"I must go," Lan Martak said, rising from the throne. He reached out and gestured with his hand to summon his light mote. It orbited in from the far reaches of the universe, ready for battle.

"What's happened?" demanded Kiska k'Adesina. "Claybore's attacking?"

"The legs. I go for them. I see how Lirory wanted to use them. It came to me—like so many other things do now."

"How? How would he have used them?"

Lan's gaze turned outward, penetrating stone and changing from physical sight to a scrying with his magical powers. The legs glowed within their individual cases, hidden away in the deepest recesses of Yerrary. Lirory Tefize had hidden them well, but Lirory had lacked Lan's power. To Lan they were apparent.

And to Claybore, as well.

"Like a battery," Lan said, starting off. Kiska trailed behind, clutching at his sleeve. He brushed her off. He started to empower a spell to freeze her to the spot, but it refused to form on his lips. The tongue resting inside his mouth felt cottony rather than metallic every time he began a spell to subdue Kiska.

"I don't understand."

"Lirory intended to place a leg at one corner of this pyramid-shaped chamber and the other leg at still another corner. The arms each went into the other corners. Sitting on his throne placed him equidistant from the four limbs. He would draw on the power focused on this special spot." Lan indicated where the throne had been before Claybore destroyed it.

"But he had the arms and legs. Why didn't he do this when he had the chance?"

Lan smiled. Everything was so obvious to him now.

"He needed one further part. Any bodily part. In the ceiling of the chamber. Placed there, it completed a pyramid of power. I suspect he desired most the Kinetic Sphere, but Claybore had retrieved that." Lan felt a passing bitterness when he realized he had allowed it to fall into Claybore's hands. "If Lirory had known I had Claybore's tongue in my mouth, he might have succeeded. Instead, he banished me, thinking the fog outside the mountain would kill me. The tongue would have sufficed as well as the Kinetic Sphere."

"He didn't sense the tongue," said Kiska in a hushed voice. She now understood, also.

"His powers were great, but not great enough. If Lirory had formed the battery of Claybore's parts, his abilities would have been enhanced to the point not even Claybore could have withstood him."

Lan laughed aloud now.

"You can defeat him, can't you?" asked Kiska.

Lan didn't answer. He didn't have to. The answer, like all else, was obvious.

"Are you able to wrest the legs from Claybore?" she pressed.

"Stay here."

"I have to be at your side," Kiska said, her voice turning shrill with urgency. The brunette forced her way up and next to Lan. He tried once more—in vain—to form the spell to hold her back. "I've come too far not to see this through to the end."

"But you—" Lan couldn't even say the words he wanted.

Kiska k'Adesina was Claybore's commandant. She commanded legions on a score of worlds and had perpetrated crimes so ghastly his mind recoiled thinking of them. Entire cities had died on the world the pair of them had walked prior to coming to Yerrary. Only one city survived— barely—when she and Claybore had finished. Kiska k'Adesina was his sworn enemy and still he not only allowed her to come with him on this most dangerous and vital of missions, but he spoke freely to her of Lirory and of the gnome mage's discovery, how he himself had come across dozens of small clues and turned them into weapons against her master, and Lan even gave her information which could be turned against him.

And he loved her.

An addict dependent on drugs, a mage linked permanently into spell dreams, a man in love. All produced the same result, and Lan Martak found himself caught in the trap. He loved Kiska k'Adesina against reason and sanity.

"Stay back. This will be dangerous. Lirory Tefize laid traps of subtle and diabolical design."

They pushed into territory alien to Lan, but he knew it as well as he did the forests on his home world. He saw, not only with eyes but with magic—and burning like a campfire in the night were Claybore's legs. Locked onto that, Lan couldn't be turned away.

"Where you go, I will," said Kiska, but her lips curled back in a sneer that Lan failed to see. Her fingers lightly stroked a dagger hilt. She started to draw the sharp-edged weapon and sink it to the hilt in the mage's broad back, but something stopped her.

The sneer turned into a broad smile. Claybore had promised that there would come a proper time for Lan Martak's death and that it would be at her hand.

CHAPTER FIFTEEN

"You can't go," cried Kiska k'Adesina, gripping at Lan's sleeve.

He shrugged her off. Even if he couldn't use magics against her—for whatever reason—he was still physically stronger. Lan Martak stopped and considered his best course of action concerning her. Was it possible to bind Kiska in such a way she couldn't follow? He made the effort and failed, not because she tried to elude him, but because his muscles began shaking as if from some huge exertion.

"Claybore has baited a trap and waits for you," Kiska told him. "You will die if you try to recover the legs."

"How do you know?" he demanded.

"It's all part of Claybore's master plan. He wants you out of the way. If you rush in foolishly, without planning, without taking enough precautions, then you will be . . . no more."

"What do you care?" Lan raged, more at his own impotence in dealing with Kiska than at the woman.

She didn't answer. He worried that this failure on his part might carry over into actual dealing with Claybore.

193

While it struck him as odd that he had come to be so closely linked emotionally with Kiska, he didn't question it deeply. Lan's true worry lay in fighting Claybore. The other mage had eons of experience to draw upon—and Lan couldn't forget the shadow hound.

The interdimensional beast had been easily dispatched, but he *felt* the complexities in the spell conjuring it up. Given the time, Claybore might summon an even more intricate monster, one not easily sent back into the nothingness between worlds.

The slightest pause, the most minute of hesitations, and he would lose this coming battle.

And at the center of it lay Claybore's legs. Lirory had died to protect his ill-gotten treasure trove of limbs. Lan did not wish to follow that path trying to obtain them for himself.

Destruction seemed the wisest course. With Claybore in possession of his arms, any chance for completing the magical battery envisioned by Lirory Tefize was at an end. Destroy the legs, destroy them for all time. He had the power to do it—as long as they weren't attached to Claybore's body.

"I know the way is dangerous. That's why I want you to stay in Lirory's chamber. It's safe there. The gnome set ward spells Claybore can circumvent—but only after some effort."

"I stay with you," Kiska maintained stoutly. Her usually brown eyes took on highlights of green from the moss glowing in the corridor, giving her an evil, alien aspect that disquieted Lan. But was he so human himself? He had come far. The Resident of the Pit and Claybore both admitted he was now immortal, thanks to the powers he had discovered. Inhuman—unhuman.

And power!

Currents of raw energy hummed and pulsed within his body. No mere human felt like this. He hadn't when he was only a hunter in the forests of his home world. He transcended the norm and developed into more—much, much more.

Lan Martak said nothing as he spun and started through the maze inside Yerrary. The gnomes had spent centuries chewing out these corridors and had created a twisting domain that was as much a part of their heritage as the forests were his. Lan quickly forgot ordinary sight and depended more and more on a magical scrying spell to lead him through the turnings.

At first he walked with faltering steps, then became more confident and strode with his usual ground-devouring pace. Kiska struggled to keep up with him but said nothing. She would doggedly follow him into the mouth of the Netherworld.

Lan's mind quickly turned from figuring out why his bitter enemy showed such devotion now to examining the hall they took. Tiny spots glowed more brilliantly in the walls than could be accounted for from the phosphorescent moss.

"Traps," he said, pointing. He knew the woman saw nothing. How could she? He was the mage. He had the power. The *power!*

Lan moved his light mote into the center of the corridor, then split it in half. Each section of his familiar blazed a fiery path for the spots on the walls. Incandescent heat filled the tiny space the instant the two motes touched stone. The trigger spell released vastly more potent magics.

"Lirory was a clever sorcerer. The true power is hidden away. Little energy is revealed, might be ignored. But once the trigger is touched, that is the result." He pointed.

Heat still billowed from the corridor, but the magical maelstrom had spent itself. Walls had turned to slag and the floor was eaten away by the intensity of the heat blast. Lan reunited his light mote, used it to smooth over the floor for Kiska's benefit, then walked on, alert for more traps.

And he found them. Subtle ones, obvious ones, traps and spells and mind-confusing paths of all varieties. After a while, it became a game to him and little more. He pitted his wit and magical ability against the now-dead sorcerer gnome. He played the game and won repeatedly. As each obstacle was overcome, he sensed a growing within himself until he could barely withstand it. The pressure of power needing to be used bloated him.

Once, he had been like Kiska and Inyx and Ducasien and all the others. Once. No longer. He had become more now. And he would strip Claybore of his power and rule along the Cenotaph Road. It was destiny. It was *his* destiny!

"The chamber we seek is near," he said.

Kiska clung to him, barely noticed. Lan Martak moved on for the final confrontation. Claybore could not permit him to enter that chamber unopposed. To do so meant the disembodied sorcerer had lost all.

A faint smile curled Lan's lips. This was the moment he had been born for.

"What!" cried Inyx. "The fool has gone off to destroy the legs without telling us?" She sagged against the wall at the enormity of what Krek told her.

"So it would seem," the spider said. "Lan Martak has developed a cockiness bordering on overconfidence. Perhaps it is due to his exposure to the fog outside."

"That's not it, Krek. There's more to it," said Ducasien. The tall man stood, hands on narrow hips, his wide shoulders almost filling an entryway. "He thinks he is invincible."

"He might be," said Inyx in a choked voice. "He might not need us any longer."

Ducasien laid his hand on the woman's shoulder, squeezing gently. She smiled wanly, putting her own hand atop his. She barely kept her sanity these days. Loving Lan put a strain on her that became harder and harder. He ignored her—and all his friends—and obviously garnered much from Kiska k'Adesina's company. Inyx tried to rationalize that this was a ploy on Lan's part, a way of getting past Claybore's guard.

She tried to believe and failed.

"Inyx," said Ducasien, "we can leave. The trip to the cenotaphs won't take long. Leave him to his little war."

"It's not little, damn it!" she flared. "This spans worlds. There's nowhere we could go and not confront Claybore if Lan should lose. We began this battle together and we'll finish it together."

"Will he accept our help?" asked Krek. "I have been guilty of choosing flight over fight in the past." The arachnid sighed like a fumarole giving vent. "Poor Klawn. Left alone because I ran like a craven from my duty. I ofttimes wonder how my hatchlings turned out. I trust they are brave spiders, one and all. Future Webmasters and mates of other Webmasters."

"Krek," Inyx said in disgust. "This is no time to reminisce."

"I was only agreeing with friend Ducasien. Lan Martak has abandoned us. Let us seek out other worlds and allow him to carry this fight to whatever finish he can."

"That's not like you," Inyx said, worried.

"He placed a geas upon me. He told me to leave him alone. I fight the magic and wonder why I bother. Even without the spell he cast upon me, weak as it is, his attitudes do much to drive me away."

Inyx had no words to answer the spider's accusation. Lan had done much to drive her away, too. In her mind she pictured vividly the sight of him making love to Kiska by the well holding the Resident of the Pit. He hadn't known she had followed, but would it have mattered to Lan? She didn't think so.

He had changed and not for the better. The power he gained corrupted him, made him brash and abrasive, too independent.

She snorted at that. How could one be too independent? Her own life had always been lived according to that notion. Now she was no longer so sure. The time with Lan had been magical, and not in terms of mere sorcery. Their bindings had emotional and mental parts mixed in with the physical.

She still loved him. But it became harder and harder to maintain that love.

"We help him. We have to," she finally said.

"Then we need a plan," spoke up Ducasien.

"This isn't your fight," she said.

"If you're there, I'm making it my fight. Now what do we need to do to prepare ourselves?"

Inyx tried to wipe away the tears forming before anyone noticed. While she was sure Krek and Ducasien both saw the motion that swiped away the salty tracks, neither mentioned it.

They called Broit Heresler into their circle and spoke quickly with the gnome. He nodded, smiled as much as he could, then went off with a few battered survivors of his clan to find the weapons needed to help Lan Martak when he finally faced Claybore.

"Through that arch," Lan Martak said, pointing. His hand glowed a dull purple in response to the ward spell Lirory Tefize had placed on the doorway. "Go through and die."

"You can take off the spell?" Kiska k'Adesina asked anxiously.

"It is a multilayered spell," he said, examining it carefully. "Very tricky. And very clever. One small slip and it is all over."

Kiska tensed, her hands balled to strike out. Lan noticed and she relaxed and let her arms hang limply at her sides. He faced the doorway and began his chants.

Slowly at first, then with increasing assurance, he peeled away the layers of the spells Lirory had wrought. Like onion skins, the spells fell away until only the bare stone archway remained. Lan wiped his sleeve over his forehead. The unlocking had taken more from him than he'd thought possible. An instant of fear flashed through him.

Was he as powerful as he thought? Did this multiple spell hold traps of which he was unaware? Had he committed too much of his power too soon? Fear chewed at his self-confidence, but he dared not admit it. Not in front of Kiska.

"Let's not tarry. We have our destiny lying in wait beyond."

With more confidence than he felt, he walked forward. Lan's eyes blinked as he passed under the stone archway. A slight electric tingle of spell had not been driven off, but it was a minor annoyance. He flicked it away as if it were nothing more than a buzzing mosquito.

He entered the chamber holding Claybore's legs.

"There they are!" cried Kiska. "Claybore's lost limbs."

Lan restrained her. She tried to bolt forward and seize the beaten copper coffins holding those legs.

"The exterior protective spells are gone. Others remain. How else could those legs stay preserved?"

"Claybore is immortal. His parts are, too."

Lan reeled at the notion. For whatever reason, this had never occurred to him. He studied the twin coffins and saw the spells woven through the fabric of metal and flesh within and knew then that Kiska was right. The spells Lirory had placed on the legs bound them to this time and place; preservation was accomplished on a more fundamental level, one fraught with magics even Lan did not pretend to understand.

"They can be destroyed," he said, more to maintain the fiction of his superiority than anything else. Showing ignorance in front of Kiska bothered him more than he cared to admit.

"Of course they can be destroyed," came a voice all too familiar from previous battlings. "You ought to know that my parts are not invincible. After all, my skin was left in a puddle of protoplasm within the Twistings."

"I wondered when you would come," said Lan, turning to face Claybore. The sorcerer stood under the archway so recently swept clear of its guardian spells.

"I waited for you to tire yourself, to do the work for me."

"I am not tired, Claybore."

"You kid yourself, then," said Claybore, laughing. His mocking gestures angered Lan, who watched as the sorcerer came into the chamber on clanking mechanical legs driven by subtle magics. The arms took up a defensive pose, ready to subvert any spell Lan might cast.

Lan savored this moment. Claybore might decry his skills, but Lan knew deep within how he had grown as a mage. Claybore was not only wrong, he was defeated and didn't know it. Lan Martak *felt* the power on him. He could not lose.

"This after you've told me it's possible to destroy your parts. Kiska was wrong. The parts are not immortal. The whole might be, but not the parts."

"Immortality rests with all the parts, but that doesn't mean the segments cannot be destroyed," said Claybore. "Left alone, they will survive for all eternity."

"Consummate magics will destroy them," said Lan, almost gloating now.

"Terrill tried and failed."

"I'm better than Terrill."

The chalk-white skull tipped sideways, the eye sockets taking on a blackness darker than space. The jaw had been destroyed and the area around the nose hole had become riddled with cracks. Claybore's skull disintegrated a bit more under each attack. Lan felt confident that he would turn the skull into dust before the day was out.

"You think so?" mocked Claybore.

"I *feel* it."

"You're a fool. You're a fool I have manipulated for my own ends for some time. You cannot win. You don't even understand what the stakes are we play for."

"Conquest. Power."

"Yes, that," said Claybore, stopping beside the copper coffin holding his left leg. "And more. Power is worthless unless it is used. And after you've conquered a few thousand worlds, what then? With immortality, mere power is not enough."

"What else can there be?" asked Lan, wondering if this was a trick to gull him into vulnerability.

"Godhood. Not only power, but the worship of all living beings. Their birth, their death, every instant in between ruled totally—by me! For millennia there has been no true god because I imprisoned the Resident of the Pit."

Lan's agile mind worked over the details and filled in gaps. It all fit a pattern. Whether what was being said was truth or not he didn't know, but it could well be. Terrill had been the Resident of the Pit's pawn in the battle against Claybore, but what was the nature of that conflict?

It had to be for the godhood Claybore mentioned. The sorcerer had dueled the reigning deity—the Resident of the Pit—and had somehow gained the upper hand. But the Resident fought back with Terrill as his principal weapon. Lacking full power, the Resident had not destroyed Claybore, but Terrill had succeeded in scattering the bodily parts along the Road.

"You get a glimmering of the truth," said Claybore. "I failed to destroy the Resident and ended up dismembered. But the Resident was unable to regain godhood because I hold him imprisoned. A stalemate lasting centuries."

"And one which is drawing to a close," said Lan. "Regaining your legs will give you the power to finally destroy the Resident. After all this time, you will be able to kill a deity."

"Yes," came the sibilant acknowledgment. "And in the

universe ruled by the god Claybore, there will be no further use for one such as yourself. Prepare to die, Lan Martak."

Lan readied himself for the battle. He stood on one side of the chamber, the coffins holding the legs between him and Claybore. All that he had gone through, the death and the misery, the pain and learning would now be put to the test.

"You will not win, Claybore," he said confidently.

The spell Claybore cast exploded like the heart of a sun, blinding him, leaving him cut free of all his senses and floating through empty infinity.

"The water you wanted," panted Broit Heresler. "We have it. But there's bad news."

Inyx looked at the tuns of acid rainwater accumulated from Eckalt's vats. How the burning quality of the water might be used, she wasn't sure, but it had to provide a potent weapon in the right circumstance.

"None of you was hurt?" she asked anxiously. She counted heads and saw Broit had returned with all the gnomes he'd set out with.

"You needed Eckalt's help, didn't you?" asked the clan leader.

"Eckalt knows more of the inner workings of Yerrary than anyone else I've met. He hops around down there, doing his work, dispensing his distilled water, and accumulating knowledge in return."

"Eckalt is dead."

"What? Claybore?" she demanded, ire rising. She had liked the toad-being. Ducasien came and laid a hand on her shoulder. She spun, even madder when she saw the man's face. It was as if he held back a secret he thought would hurt her. That failure of trust added fuel to the fire of her anger.

"Not Claybore," said Broit Heresler. "Lan Martak. He killed Eckalt without remorse. There were witnesses. Several of the Wartton clan saw it all. Martak lifted Eckalt with a spell and hurled him into the well where you say this Resident thing lives."

"Lan gave the blood sacrifice," Inyx said in a choked voice. "He sacrificed an intelligent being. Eckalt was such a harmless little creature."

"He murdered Eckalt, is what he did," said Broit Heresler. "And he didn't even leave us a proper body to bury. That might not be such a loss, though, if we can create another cenotaph because of it. A new way on and off the world is always a boon. New travelers, new corpses to bury. There's usually a way to turn trouble into gain, especially if you're clever like I am."

"But he could have sensed Eckalt's intelligence," she said.

"He didn't even try," said Ducasien. "I already knew but didn't want to say anything. He is a callous killer, this friend of yours."

"There is nothing wrong in that," cut in Krek, "but the circumstances hardly warranted it. Lan Martak could have spent a few more minutes looking for an appropriate sacrifice to awaken the Resident."

"The power has gone to his head. He thinks only of himself, that he is invincible," declared Ducasien.

"You're still thinking to help this corpse-destroyer?" asked Broit. "Not that it's any cause for alarm, as long as he creates enough business for us Hereslers."

"I say we consecrate the cenotaph to Eckalt, then leave this world," said Ducasien.

"Friend Ducasien has a point," said Krek. The spider bobbed up and down, then added, "However, we know only one side of this issue. Should we not query Lan Martak first? While he has sorely mistreated me, my innate sense of fair play comes to the fore. In the past we owed him much. Surely, we can ask and listen to his explanation."

Inyx saw all eyes on her. The decision rested squarely

on her shoulders whether they were to carry out the planned attack in conjunction with Lan's magical assault or simply turn and leave Yerrary and this world.

Ducasien wanted to leave. Krek asked for answers from Lan.

Her vote decided the issue.

"You recovered nicely, Martak," congratulated Claybore. But the younger mage did not take it as a compliment. To do so meant Claybore gained a fraction of power over him.

Spinning through space—blinded and deaf, totally without senses—had startled him, but fear wasn't his response. He had fought and found within himself the right ways of countering Claybore's attack.

He whirled back and still faced Claybore. No time had elapsed. The wild flight had been entirely illusory—but ever so real while he was caught up in the spell.

"A petty trick," he said, knowing how Claybore had done it. "Goodbye."

The spell he cast contained elements of the most powerfull spells he was capable of controlling. The invisible web caught at Claybore and further cracked the skull, a piece falling to the stone floor. Lan tightened and the magics spilled over from the edge of his control and eroded away the coffin immediately in front of Claybore.

That almost proved his undoing.

The leg, freed of the magical bindings Lirory Tefize had placed upon it, kicked out of the copper coffin and balanced in a mockery of life on the floor. The sight of the dismembered leg moving of its own volition startled Lan into relaxing his attack.

And when Claybore riposted, it came in an unexpected fashion. The leg hopped forward and kicked straight for Lan's groin. The physical pain meant little to Lan; the shock of seeing the leg attack allowed cracks to develop in his own defenses.

Claybore entered that breach easily. The spells used by the mage beat at Lan's every vulnerable point. He was forced backward, driven to the wall. The inner core on which he relied came to his aid, giving him the respite to reform his defenses.

All the while the ghastly leg continued to hop and kick at him.

"See, Martak? All of me wants to see you die," said Claybore. "And you will—you will die as only an immortal can. You will live forever and be in complete pain for all eternity. Nothing will save you. You will cry in the dark for surcease and never find it. You will die, not in body, but in mind. Die, Martak, die!"

Lan couldn't stop the surging attack, but he could turn it aside enough to keep from succumbing. And knowing his strength was nowhere near adequate to destroy Claybore as he'd thought, cunning took over. Lan Martak turned aside the assault and redirected it for the hopping, kicking leg.

"No!" came the shriek as Claybore realized what was happening.

His leg vanished in a sizzling cloud of greasy black smoke, lost forever.

"Your skin is gone. I have your tongue. Now your leg is destroyed. Who is losing, Claybore?"

Lan twisted away as heat destroyed the other copper coffin. Droplets of molten metal seared his skin, raised blisters, burned like a million ants devouring his flesh. The other leg bounded free of its vaporized coffin and went hopping toward Claybore.

Lan tried to stop it and found the other sorcerer's spells prevented it. Leg and torso would soon be reunited. What power would this give Claybore? Lan didn't want to find out.

"You can't stop me, Martak," gloated Claybore. "You had your chance. You've failed."

"Aren't you the one failing, Claybore? Where's your

right leg? It's gone. Completely destroyed. The other soon will be."

"Never!"

Lan sent out tangling spells to numb the nerves in the leg. They failed. The leg did not live in the same way other things did. He hurled fireballs and sent elementals and opened pits and still he failed to prevent the inexorable movement of the left leg as it hopped toward Claybore.

Every spell he wove sapped that much more strength from him. Lan realized with a sick feeling that Claybore was growing stronger. When the leg rejoined, his power would be supreme.

Lan was lost. The universe was lost—and ruling over it would be a new god: Claybore.

CHAPTER SIXTEEN

Lan Martak fought with all the ferocity of a cornered rat. Try as he would, however, Claybore always proved the stronger. Lan thought he had strength and youth on his side; Claybore's primary advantage was experience that sapped Lan's strength, made him commit to foolish attacks using his spells so that they were sent skittering off harmlessly.

Lan felt weakness again. His hands shook and his vision blurred. But he all too clearly saw that Claybore's left leg hopped toward the sorcerer. In only seconds the limb would be rejoined. Claybore would have triumphed to that extent—and it might be enough to bring his evil plans to fruition.

"All the universe will be mine to rule," came Claybore's mocking words, so soft and sibilant that they were almost a whisper. "More than ruling, all the peoples of those worlds will worship me. I shall reign supreme forever!"

"Won't that pall on you?" gasped out Lan. He countered a nerve-numbing spell and started a chant of his own to renew his attack. Power slipped from him like a dropped cloak. Grabbing at it only caused it to slide away faster.

"Ask me in a million years."

"You'll ruin worlds."

"Yes."

"You don't care. You owe it to the people you'll rule not to harm them."

"Why?" Then Claybore's laughter echoed in Lan's skull. "Your tone has changed, Martak. Now you're trying to invest me with a conscience. You're admitting I have won. It is apparent, isn't it?"

"Yes," Lan grated out—but he had one last spell to try. Lirory Tefize had recorded this one and Lan had not dared use it. The binding spell holding Claybore's arms and legs had been potent. Would it still work and would it work on Claybore himself?

Lan began the motions with his fingers. The air twisted into improbable shapes before him. The words formed colored threads in the midst of the writhing mass. And he sent his light mote directly into the vortex to supply power.

The virtually uncontrolled spell burst forth with more vehemence than Lan had anticipated—or Claybore expected.

The sorcerer screamed as his leg froze in midhop and fell lifeless to the stone floor. His rejoined arms began twitching spastically and Lan watched in fascination as the Kinetic Sphere, Claybore's very heart, began pushing outward from his chest. But the spell was not without effect on Lan himself. His mouth turned metallic and his tongue began to glow hotter and hotter. Lirory's spell affected *all* of Claybore's bodily parts, and that included Claybore's tongue.

"You can't do this!" shrieked Claybore. The ghastly apparition of the sorcerer leaped and cavorted about, dodging unseen menace. The cracks in the skull deepened until Lan wondered how it held together. With the jawbone already gone, Claybore turned even more gruesome with every passing moment.

Lan found himself unable to speak, but the sensation of

victory assuaged that. Claybore was becoming wrapped in the spell and would soon lie as numbed on the floor as his left leg. No longer even kicking, the leg presented no menace at all. Its magics were contained. And Claybore would be soon, also.

Lan blinked in surprise when all the magical attack against him suddenly ceased. His tongue still burned, but that was the product of his own conjuring.

"Given up so easily, Claybore?" he croaked out. Then Lan saw what the sorcerer did. The attack hadn't lessened, it had shifted.

Kiska k'Adesina writhed on the floor, face blue from the spells cutting off her air. Her body arched violently as if her back would snap, then she flopped onto her belly and fingers cut into stone as she tried to escape Claybore's punishment.

"Stop it!" cried Lan.

Without thinking, he directed his full power to shielding the woman from Claybore. The instant his attack on Claybore stopped, the disembodied sorcerer countered.

"You can't let her come to harm, can you, Martak?" chided Claybore. "You love her. You *must* protect her. You have to. She means more than your own life, doesn't she?"

"No," said Lan. The weakness of his reply told him everything. He did love Kiska k'Adesina, his sworn enemy, the woman who hated him with an obsession bordering on insanity; he loved her.

"I see it in your face. Defend her. Keep her from harm."

Claybore's spells trapped the woman on the floor like a bug with a pin through it. She gasped for breath, twisted about as joints snapped and limbs turned in ways never intended. Lan watched as Claybore broke her physically with his powerful spells.

But if he protected Kiska adequately, he left himself open to attack. One or the other it was possible to defend, but not both of them.

"She dies, Martak. Your lover dies."

The desolation welling up within Lan couldn't be expressed. He had no true love for Kiska. She had tried to kill him on more occasions than he could count, yet he did love her. Irrationally, without any regard for Inyx or his feelings for her, Lan loved Kiska.

"Look at her pain, Martak. I really don't want to do this to her, but it gives me some practice. When I become a true god, I think I shall do this every day."

Lan gambled everything on forming one last spell to hurl every spark of energy he had directly at Claybore—to stun Claybore, to stop the torture Kiska felt.

The bolt lashed forth with such intensity the rock walls turned viscid and flowed in sluggish molten streams. The dancing light mote guided the tip of this energy blast directly for Claybore's skull. The sorcerer staggered back, his metallic legs beginning to melt under the onslaught. But the reaction was not that which Lan expected. Claybore was being driven to the wall and yet an aura of triumph surrounded him.

"Stop her!" came Krek's voice. Lan ventured a quick glance to one side and saw Kiska k'Adesina rising up, dagger in hand. And the dagger was aimed straight for Lan's back.

As long as he maintained the spell against Claybore, Lan couldn't move, couldn't defend himself against physical attack. Even worse than this was the sight of the woman he loved trying to kill him, as if she still plotted with Claybore for his downfall.

Inyx rushed forward, quick, strong hand gripping Kiska's wrist and twisting at the last possible instant. Lan felt hot steel rake over his back. Thick streams of blood gushed forth, but the wound was messier than it was dangerous.

But the shock of seeing the woman he loved try to kill him broke the continuity of his spell. Claybore began magically worming free of the attack.

"Come," the sorcerer hissed. "Come to me!"

The leg, once numbed, now twitched and kicked and bobbed until it was again hopping across the chamber. Lan's power waned; he was unable to cope with Inyx and Kiska fighting, the spell he launched against Claybore and the countering spell the sorcerer returned, and the sight of the leg hopping to rejoin the body.

"Krek," he moaned. "The leg. Stop it!"

Krek's huge front leg reached out and batted away the leg, sending it into the far wall. Flesh hissed slightly as it touched rock already turned molten from other spells.

"The heat. Oh, my precious fur is smoldering," cried the spider.

"Never mind that. Stop the leg from reaching Claybore."

Lan's words needed more conviction to get the spider to move. The way the man's tongue burned within his mouth told him that his own enervating spell had been turned against him. Claybore's cunning played on his every weakness, his every mistake.

But if Krek was unable to move, Broit Herseler and his few surviving clansmen did act. They rushed into the chamber, spades and picks cutting and hacking at the leg. The limb tried valiantly to defend itself against the tiny chunks being taken out of it, but there were too many gnomes attacking.

Claybore cursed, tried to blast the gnomes, and found himself overextended. He dared not relent in his attack on Lan; to do so meant his own demise. But he needed his leg and the gnomes prevented it from rejoining him.

"Bring out the water," Broit called. Others of the grave-digger clan rolled huge barrels into the room.

"You can't do that!" shrieked Claybore.

They threw the acid rainwater onto the leg. Flesh smoldered and turned putrescent. Soon, only the bare leg bones remained, and they were easily hammered into dust by the gnomes.

"You've lost, Claybore," said Lan. "Stop your drive for

power now. We can work out some sort of truce."

"Truce? You fool! You don't understand. I've tasted ultimate power. I can't turn away from it. I can't share it."

The sorcerer lay in a heap on the ground, his metallic legs destroyed and his own legs unreachable now. Lan Martak had magically blasted the right leg and the left was little more than bonemeal in a paste of acid water on the floor.

Claybore reached up and touched the spot on his chest where the Kinetic Sphere pinkly pulsed.

"You will find this victory fleeting, Martak," promised Claybore. The sorcerer's entire body blinked out of existence.

"You killed him!" cried Broit Heresler, jumping up and down.

"He shifted worlds," Lan said in a tired voice. "We stopped him from regaining either of his legs, but he still walks the Road, plotting and planning."

A strangled sound came to the mage's ears. Lan spun and saw Inyx with her fingers firmly wrapped around Kiska's throat. The dark-haired woman slowly choked the life from her victim.

"Inyx, no!" he cried. Ducasien placed a hand on Lan's shoulder to restrain him. Lan cast a minor spell that hurled Ducasien across the room. A second spell sent Inyx after him, leaving Kiska alone and gasping for air on the floor. He went to her and knelt, cradling her head in his lap.

Emotions boiled within him. He hated her for all she had done. She was insane, a cold-blooded murderer. And he loved her. He had to protect her at all costs.

"Lan Martak," came Krek's voice, "she attempted to stab you in the back. You saw. You know of her treachery."

"I love her," he choked out. His heart leaped with joy when he saw her pale brown eyes flicker open and focus on him. Lan read only hatred blazing up at him and it didn't matter. He loved her.

"Claybore has cast some sort of geas on you," said Krek.

"Examine yourself, Lan Martak, or beware."

Lan Martak looked up at the spider, not understanding.

"Friend Ducasien, do you mind if I accompany you?" asked Krek.

"You're not staying with him?" asked Inyx.

"I have decided that it is impossible for me to bear his silliness any further," said Krek, a tear forming in his eye. "You are my friends. No longer can I name Lan Martak that."

Inyx rubbed a spot on Krek's leg and said, "You can come along. We don't know exactly where we're headed, but it has to be a place better than this."

The plains stretching out from the foot of Yerrary were wracked with winds and the acid rain pelted down, forming tiny blazes wherever it touched. Broit Heresler and several of his gravediggers were escorting them to the graveyard. With Claybore driven off and the Tefize clan leaderless, Broit had stepped into the power vacuum and assumed control of most of the inner workings of Yerrary.

"It is a duty I take seriously," the gnome declared. "Imagine the bodies to be buried. Yerrary will function as it never has before!" His clan had cheered this, but Inyx found scant pleasure in it.

Lan Martak insisted on pursuing Claybore. She agreed with that. She couldn't force herself to accompany the man any further as long as he insisted on keeping Kiska k'Adesina by his side.

"It is a spell of subtle power," said Krek, seeing her frown. "But it is one I cannot cope with, either."

She hugged Krek's leg and then turned. Ducasien waited just outside the doorway. They began their trek across the plains for the cenotaphs opening and closing in the graveyard. Inyx didn't know what world they would end up on. And it didn't matter.

Halfway to the grave site she turned and looked back at

the black mass of Yerrary. A small figure stood atop the mountain, bathed in white fire. She lifted her hand, started to wave, then jerked around. Even if Lan watched, it was a show of weakness to make any gesture.

"You still love him, don't you?" asked Ducasien.

"No."

"You don't lie well," the man said. He looked toward Yerrary and the white pillar of fire, heaved a sigh, and then hugged Inyx close. She buried her face in his shoulder and sobbed quietly.

"A cenotaph opens," said Krek, pointing with one of his back legs. The spider watched the two humans enter and wink out of existence on this world and go to another. He nodded to Broit Heresler, then climbed into the cenotaph and followed his friends. Somehow, the shifting from one world to another didn't ease the pain or remove the tears forming in the spider's huge eyes.

The last thing he heard was the sound of Broit Heresler's picks working on the stony ground to dig new graves.

"Good riddance," snarled Kiska k'Adesina. She stood close beside Lan Martak on the mountaintop. The circle of energy surrounding them held the acid rain and the mind-altering fog at bay. Lan had had enough experience with both and knew better than to tempt fate without magical protection.

The tiny procession wended its way across the barren plain to the graveyard. Lan watched and felt a coldness inside grow until he wanted to scream. Inyx gone. Krek gone.

He clenched his fists and shook with emotion.

"You don't need them. You have me. What were they, anyhow? A slut and an overgrown bug. You love me, Lan my darling. We can rule together."

"Be quiet," he said. Kiska only laughed at him, knowing his impotence in dealing with her.

The cenotaph blinked open. Lan watched the magics that

linked one world to another begin to flow. First one brighter spot, then another and finally a third and last. Inyx. Ducasien. Krek. Gone.

All that remained on this world was the burning ground where the rains washed over the stone.

"Claybore must be destroyed," he said.

"Yes, my love," came Kiska's mocking words.

Lan Martak clapped his hands and summoned his new-found power to shift worlds without a cenotaph or the Kinetic Sphere. He didn't need Inyx or Krek. Claybore would be stopped.

A second clap of his hands prepared the world-spanning bridge of magic.

He would stop Claybore and rule a million worlds.

On the third clap of his hands, only barren rock remained where he and Kiska had stood. They now walked a lush, green meadow on a world distant in space and time.

BEST-SELLING
Science Fiction
and
Fantasy